(winner of the Hawthornden Prize and the Ruth Hadden Memorial Award), *In a Land of Plenty* (made into a ten-part BBC series), *Landed* (shortlisted for the IMPAC Dublin Literary Award and the Royal Society of Literature Ondaatje Prize, winner of the MJA Open Book Awards) and most recently the critically acclaimed West Country Trilogy. He has been Writer in Residence at Cheltenham Festival of Literature and a Royal Literary Fund Fellow. He has taught creative writing for Arvon, the University of Oxford, First Story and Ruskin College, among others, and mentored for Gold Dust. He is a Fellow of the Royal Society of Literature, and has been the recipient of a Lannan Award. He and his wife live in Oxford. They have two children.

CHEMISTRY
and Other Stories

Tim Pears

BLOOMSBURY PUBLISHING
LONDON · OXFORD · NEW YORK · NEW DELHI · SYDNEY

BLOOMSBURY PUBLISHING
Bloomsbury Publishing Plc
50 Bedford Square, London, WC1B 3DP, UK
29 Earlsfort Terrace, Dublin 2, Ireland

BLOOMSBURY, BLOOMSBURY PUBLISHING and the Diana logo are
trademarks of Bloomsbury Publishing Plc

First published in Great Britain 2021
This edition published 2022

A catalogue record for this book is available from the British Library

ISBN: HB: 978-1-5266-2337-9; PB: 978-1-5266-2341-6;
EBOOK: 978-1-5266-2339-3; EPDF: 978-1-5266-4530-2

2 4 6 8 10 9 7 5 3 1

Typeset by Integra Software Services Pvt. Ltd.
Printed and bound in Great Britain by CPI Group (UK) Ltd, Croydon CR0 4YY

MIX
Paper from
responsible sources
FSC® C171272

To find out more about our authors and books visit www.bloomsbury.com
and sign up for our newsletters

For Jane, Greta and Stewart,
West Country comrades

CONTENTS

How to Tell a Short Story

Jane came back from the bar carrying a glass of white wine for me in one hand and a Campari and soda in the other.

'I've got an idea for a short story,' I told her.

'Finally,' she replied. 'A short story. After all those endless novels. Thank you, God.'

'It's a good idea.'

'Tell me.'

'A lad begs his dad to lend him the car,' I began. 'The dad makes him promise to be careful, not to drink anything, the lad's only recently passed his test.'

'I like it,' Jane said. 'As a reader, I'm thinking: this car is going to bring trouble. It's a smoking gun.'

'Don't you mean a loaded gun?'

'A smoking car. Smoke pouring from the engine, at the side of the road.'

'I was thinking more in terms of a terrible accident than a simple breakdown.'

'You would.'

'The poor father, his guilt, the mother accusing him, "Why did you let our son borrow the car, you fool? You killer." The after-effects on the marriage. On siblings.'

'Yes, Timmy, that's your kind of story. But all sorts of other, less drastic things could happen. Maybe the lad gives someone a lift, or agrees to drop something off for some dodgy character. He's stopped by the police. Arrested. The drug dealers—'

'Who said anything about drugs?'

'Okay,' Jane said. 'Arms dealers. They think he's going to spill the beans, even though we know he knows nothing. They reckon he's a grass. A snitch.'

'He comes out on bail.'

'A marked man. And not just him. Since you always want to bring your stories round to families. His whole family are in danger!'

'It's a perilous situation for everyone.'

Jane sipped her Campari. I drank my wine.

'To be honest,' she said, 'I prefer love stories. Couldn't he borrow the car to impress a girl? Or better, a boy?'

'You incurable romantic.'

'It all goes wrong. Maybe they drive into the night, the car breaks down, miles from anywhere, they lose each other, there's all sorts of fraught incidents but in the end it all goes right.'

'Sounds great,' I said, 'but can we get back to my story? I want to tell you about the terrible accident.

The whole point's about how I describe it. In forensic detail.'

'Like *The Pier Falls*?'

'Sure. You remember that awful pile-up on the M5 a few years ago?'

Jane grimaced. 'He's just passed his test and you're going to send him up the motorway?'

'H'm. You might have a point.'

'I need a smoke,' Jane said. 'I think there's a beer garden.'

I got us more drinks and joined her outside, where she was rolling a cigarette.

'I've been thinking,' she said.

'It's probably the nicotine.'

'I haven't inhaled yet. Look at me. I haven't even licked the paper.'

'Just the prospect of nicotine set your nerves jangling, brain racing.'

'Yeh, whatever.' Jane lit her rollie, exhaled and said, 'Let's go back to the set-up. The car's great, but the dad and his lad, that's such a cliché, Tim. A man and his precious vehicle; boy racer, can't help himself. Bound to be trouble. Too obvious.'

'Thanks.'

'But I like the car. Let's think a bit more about the people and their relationship.'

We sat in silence for a while. I opened a packet of peanuts I'd bought. Jane smoked.

'I suppose we could make the lad a lass,' I said.

'I've got it!' Jane said. 'We make the lad a nineteen-year-old girl. But she's the one with the car. It's hers and she's lending it.'

'She's lending her car to her out-of-work father? Remember *Raining Stones*? When the girl gives her dad a fiver?'

'Ricky Tomlinson, yeh.'

'That scene. It kills me, even now, just to think about it.'

'It's good.'

'I think it's one of my favourite scenes in cinema. Even though Ken Loach—'

'Don't start criticising Ken Loach, for fuck's sake.'

'Okay. All right. No need to get antsy.'

'I'm just saying. Leave him out of it.'

'Okay,' I agreed. 'So, maybe a daughter and her father ... '

'Grandfather.'

'What?'

'The girl lives with her mother and the mother's father.'

'I could go with that. But I do actually need a sibling too, maybe the girl has a brother.'

'A stepbrother. It's a blended family.'

'Possibly.'

'But the stepfather's buggered off.'

'Just like the father did.'

'No, the father topped himself.'

'Jesus, Jane.'

'Now I think about it, the grandfather is not the mother's father, he's her father-in-law.'

'The girl's father's father or the stepbrother's father's father?'

'No need to be facetious, lovey. I'm just trying to help make your story more realistic. A bit less *middle-class happy family is slightly unhappy about something*. What did Pawel say about your fiction?'

'That was years ago.'

'What did he say?'

'He said that I do understand stories are about conflict, it's just that mine are about conflict between nice people and nicer people.'

'Ouch. Did he really say that?'

'It was five novels ago. I'm over it. So, this girl's got her shiny, cool Mini, that she's very proud and protective of, but Grandad wants to borrow it. Why?'

'To impress some old floozy, of course. Or better, some old chap. At the age of eighty, Grandad's coming out. In a pink Mini.'

'You and your bloody love stories. Okay, so the old dear lives a few miles up the motorway.'

'Please, Tim,' Jane said. 'Don't kill these two love-birds off. We've only just met them.'

'Best time to kill them off then, before the reader gets too attached.'

Jane frowned, nodding. 'Wait. I like that idea, that the reader develops feelings just as Grandad develops feelings. You might want to rewrite the beginning with that in mind.'

I shook my head. 'This is not a romance, Jane. I'm sorry. Grandad borrows his granddaughter's—'

'Or step-granddaughter's—'

'—pride and joy, a pink Mini, and sets off ... '
I paused.

'Yes,' Jane said, 'I'm with you. Carry on.'

'Hang on,' I said. 'If Grandad dies in a shocking car accident, it's not such a terrible thing as if a teenager dies. It won't destroy the family.'

'Mum would be a little sad but also relieved,' Jane agreed.

'One could almost say that the girl's loss of her precious car would be a greater tragedy, or have a greater impact, than the death of this old man.'

'He had a good life,' Jane said. 'A good innings.' She lit another cigarette. 'I see him as a cricketer in his youth, actually. Dashing in white flannels. On the village green.' She spotted me looking askance at her and said, 'Flashback scene. In the TV version.'

'You want to option it?' I asked.

'I know someone who might,' she said. 'But it needs a bit more ... '

'More what?'

'Romance,' she said, laughing. 'I need a wee. I'll get another round.'

While Jane was gone, I rolled a cigarette, telling myself it was for her. When she came back, I told her I'd had a breakthrough. 'The old boy's got a secret,' I said.

'You mean apart from his sexual orientation?' Jane asked. 'Good. Secrets in stories are good.'

'If he reveals the secret, it will cause him pain, shame, disgrace, but he'll be rewarded with money, which he wants to give to his daughter-in-law and step-grand-daughter and step-grandson.'

'And he needs a car for this?'

'Yes,' I said, though I was bluffing somewhat. I mean, he could have taken public transport, I imagine, or a taxi, or hitch-hiked. 'He drives out of town,' I resumed, 'to a large country house. There he asks to see Lady Whatsit, landowner. She graciously invites him to her drawing room. Coffee and biscuits are brought. He tells her that as a young man he was an assistant gardener here, and he had a clandestine affair with the Duke's daughter, impregnating her with ... Her Ladyship with whom he now speaks.'

Jane stared at me, clearly sceptical.

'You wanted romance,' I said.

'That was romance?' she asked. 'A fumble in the green-house between a gardening lad and an aristocrat lass?'

I ignored her and continued. 'Her Ladyship is outraged, and throws him out. As she does so he offers to take a DNA test to prove it. That gives her pause. She watches him drive away—'

'In the pink Mini.'

'On the way home, he's involved in a terrible accident.'

Jane groaned. 'You just won't let it go.'

'It's okay,' I said. 'No gruesome detail, I promise. But a young man passes the scene of the accident – lights flashing, sirens blaring – he sees a body covered up beside this mangled pink Mini, and tells his mother what he saw when he gets home.'

'Don't tell me,' Jane said, 'his mother is Her Ladyship.'

'Precisely,' I said. 'Her Ladyship rushes to the kitchen, where she finds the cook about to wash up. Just in time, she grabs the coffee mug the old boy was drinking from, and sends it off for DNA analysis, during which time she finds out from newspaper reports of the fatal car accident who he was, where he lived.'

'Meanwhile the family are grieving.'

'Right. They have a funeral for the old boy.'

'Tell me the girl gets a new Mini. The old one was insured, right?'

'Sadly, no,' I said. 'I'm sorry, Jane. It was only insured for the girl to drive. In fact, the only way she avoids prosecution for allowing an uninsured person to drive her car is by claiming that her grandfather stole it.'

'That's really sad.'

'It is.' We sat in silence a moment, absorbing what it must mean to tell the world your deceased grandfather was a common thief. I guess we were both a little inebriated by this point. 'So now,' I continued, 'the girl and her mother, and maybe stepbrother, are bereaved and impoverished.'

'And carless,' Jane said, with feeling. She loves her old yellow Polo.

'But it's okay,' I assured her. 'Because Her Ladyship, who's fabulously wealthy, gives them a great wad of money.'

'They're family.'

'No, they're not, actually. The DNA test came back negative. The old boy and Her Ladyship are unrelated. Maybe her flighty mother was also having a thing with the butler. But she was touched by the story, by his love for her mother, and by his death.'

'Although,' Jane said, 'the story might not have been true, right? He might have been an old fraudster. I mean, who's telling the story anyway? Is the narrator reliable?'

'That's a good question,' I said. 'We'll come to it. Meanwhile, Her Ladyship sends her son round with the money.'

'The son who saw the aftermath of the car accident?'

'The very one. He knocks on the door. The girl answers. Their eyes meet. And that's it. *Coup de foudre*.'

'Too obvious,' Jane said.

'Love at first sight is never obvious!' I objected. 'And we never tire of it.'

'I mean the girl is too obvious,' she said. 'It should be the stepbrother.'

I laughed. 'You don't give up,' I said.

'Who, by the way, to add a further authenticating complication, is trans.'

'Okay,' I said. 'I can go with that. So now we have: the mother is no longer poor, the girl has a new car, the boy – the transgender stepbrother – is in love. It's a good start.'

'A start?' Jane said, horrified. 'What do you mean, a start? That's an ending to a short story if ever I heard one.'

'Do you mind if I smoke your cigarette?' I said. 'I'm beginning to think it's a novel. Wait till you hear Chapter Two.'

'Oh, good grief,' she said.

Blue

He knew he'd died at three o'clock in the afternoon of Wednesday, July the 29th, 1988, the moment he woke up in the room that he'd come to hate. He hadn't left it for two months now, and he was wearily familiar not only with every object – with the thermometer in a glass beside the lamp and the heavy chest of drawers and the dark, forbidding wardrobe – but also with the quality of light and shadow according to what time of day it was; the way the room expanded and contracted as the ceiling joists shrank at night and swelled during the day; and how sound changed at different times so that in the morning his voice was dulled and barely reached the door, but in the dark the room became an echo chamber, his daughter's name, *Joan*, rebounding off the walls and returning to him from many different directions.

He was familiar with all these things but none of them interested him, as he declined in the starched sheets, propped up against a backrest of awkward, misshapen pillows that his daughter regularly thumped and plumped up with a ritualised but desolate enthusiasm, as if doing with them what she wished she could do for her father. He'd gradually lost his huge rustic appetite until it had become a torment to swallow even the soups and junkets she prepared in the liquidiser, and he lost weight with inexorable logic until the once robust farmer was a skinny wraith whose ribs were showing for the first time in fifty years.

The pain moved around his body like a poacher in the night searching for a vulnerable deer in the pinewoods. It had first attacked him in his heel, reappeared in his neck, then after a six-month respite erupted from deep cover in his back, to roam up and down his spine with sporadic, intense malevolence. He knew (and so did everyone else) that it had to be lung cancer, since he'd smoked sixty untipped cigarettes a day since the age of fourteen; so why the hell didn't it just eat up his lungs and have done with it?

The pain was what had wrecked him. Joseph had always thought he was impervious to pain and his grandson, Michael, had grown up in awe of his grandfather's disdain of both the occasional accident and the regular discomfort that beset the life of a farmer. When he gashed his hand or banged his head he only bothered to use his handkerchief if the blood was making too much of a mess of everything. And when they'd unclogged the field drains the previous February, while Mike was whimpering like a child from the cold, his grandfather thrust his arms into icy mud as if oblivious to reality.

But this pain was different: it gripped him in its teeth like a primitive dog, and there was neither escape nor end to its torture. He felt nauseous. He fantasised heating up a kitchen knife and cutting out whole afflicted chunks of his own flesh, that that might bring relief – but he couldn't even reach the stairs. Dr Buckle prescribed ever-changing drugs of increasing dosage, until the pain was dulled and so were all his senses and he found himself withdrawing into a small space where there was no sense and no sensation, only a vague disgust with the faint remaining evidence of a world he'd once inhabited with force and command.

Joseph Howard knew he'd died at three o'clock in the afternoon when he woke from his inconclusive nap and he looked around the room with a sharpness of vision that made his mind collapse backwards through the years, because he'd refused to wear spectacles and hadn't seen the world as clearly as this since his fortieth birthday. He could read the hands of the alarm clock without holding it three inches in front of his face, he could make out each stem and petal in the blue floral wallpaper, and the edges of things were miraculous in their definition, lifting away from each other and occupying their own precise space instead of merging into a dull stew of objects.

He pricked up his ears and heard a voice outside call-ing, and although it was too far away for him to make out the actual words he could recognise, beyond any doubt, the tone and inflection of his grandson, Mike. And even more remarkably, when another man's voice answered, from even further away, he knew that that was old Freemantle's grandson, Tom.

It was then that he realised, too, that the pain had gone. His whole body ached with something simi-lar to the symptoms of flu, as if his body had been punched in his sleep; but it was such a contrast to the agony of these last months that he felt on top of the world. He got out of bed and stood up, and the blood drained from his head and made him feel woozy, so he sat back down to get his balance. Yet it was actu-ally pleasurable to come so close to passing out. It made him recall the one time he had ever fainted, as a beansprouting adolescent in the farmyard, the world suddenly losing its anchorage and swooning deliri-ously out of control.

Joseph had finished dressing and was tying his shoe-laces, with an infant's concentration, when his daughter came into the room carrying a mug of weak tea. 'Father!' she cried. 'What on earth's you think you're doing?' She rushed around the side of the bed but he took no notice of her until he'd finished, and then he sat up and looked her in the eyes and said, 'Joan, I feels better and I'm getting up.' Then his smile disappeared and he studied her face with a scrutiny that she found unnerv-ing, taking in the crow's feet and the puffiness around her eyes and the small lines at each side of her mouth, and he said, 'You're a good girl, Joan.'

He knew he'd died but he didn't care. He found his stick behind the door and went for a walk into the village. He could feel his blood flow thin through his veins and his left hip no longer troubled him. He passed two or three people on his way to the shop and they returned his cheerful greeting with manifest surprise and a certain awkwardness.

The shop bell rang and Elsie came through from the kitchen. Her large owl's eyes widened behind her thick pebble-specs, and then narrowed. 'Does Joan know you's out, Joseph?' she demanded suspiciously. 'She was only in yere just now.'

'Don't worry about me, Elsie,' he replied, 'I never felt better. Only I wants some fags. I've not had a smoke in ages.'

Elsie looked away, embarrassed. 'I haven't got none of your sort in, Joseph. You's the only one what smoked that brand.' She reached over to the shelves. 'You could try some of this, they says 'tis a strong one.'

'I'm not bothered, I'll take a packet of they,' he smiled. She handed them to him hurriedly and he felt in his pockets. 'Damn it,' he said, 'I've come out without any money. You know how much I hates credit, but can I send the lad down later on?'

'Course you can, bay,' she said without looking at him, 'you git on, now.'

As he turned to leave, he said, 'I might even bring it myself.'

Dr Buckle appeared the next day and took his temperature and checked his pulse and listened to the sounds of his insides through the dangling stethoscope. Then he declared, in a voice of scientific indifference, 'It's an impressive respite, Joseph. But you're still weak. Don't overdo it.'

He wanted to get straight back out on the farm, but Joan told Mike she'd hold him responsible if Joseph picked up so much as an ear of corn, so he left his grandfather behind in the yard. Joseph wandered around the garden and poked about in the sheds. It was a hot day, the sun rose high in a blue sky, and he wiped the sweat from his neck and forehead. Sparrows swooped in and out of the eaves, a throstle sang from one of the apple trees, and when he saw a magpie in the first field he knew without any doubt that he'd see another, and sure enough there it was over by the hedge.

A ladybird landed on the back of his hand. At first the tiny creature appeared strange, only for being so distinct in his cleansed vision, but then he observed that its markings were red dots on a black shell instead of the usual other way round. He didn't think he'd ever seen one like that before, but he might well have and never been struck by it. There must be a name for it, he thought: an inverted ladybird, perhaps; a topsy-turvy.

He lifted his hand and blew, and the delicate insect opened its wings and flew away.

During the months of his miserable decline Joan had climbed uncomplaining up the stairs many times a day to make him comfortable, to help him on to the bedpan and carry it off to the bathroom, to rub cream into his dry skin, eventually to spoon food into his mouth. His recovery must have meant a great easing of her burden and he was frankly glad that she let him occupy himself now without interruption. Midway through the afternoon he became aware of a curious, pleasing sensation somewhere inside him and then he realised with surprise what it was: hunger. He marched into the kitchen.

'You'll not believe this, girl, but I've got myself an appetite all of a sudden.'

Joan didn't look at him directly but fussed around in the fridge and said at the same time, 'Sit down, I'll knock 'e up a sandwich.'

Joseph planted himself at the table and laid his cigarettes and matches on its grainy surface. He could remember his own father making it, after a huge old beech tree had come down in an April gale. He could remember the sweet smell of the shavings as his father sawed and planed in the far shed, and he could remember the way his father kept nails between his moist lips.

Joan set a plate of sliced white-bread sandwiches in front of him and murmured that she was off shopping, as she departed from the room. He watched her through the window disappear down the lane and then he closed his eyes, the better to appreciate the texture of mushy bread and coarse ham, and to savour the sharp distraction of mustard, contradicted by granules of demerara sugar.

That evening after supper Joseph suggested a game of draughts with Mike, and they played for the first time since Mike was a child and Joseph had taught him, after the boy's father had left. They played half a dozen games, all of which Mike spent hunched over the board uneasily, never once looking up at his grandfather, who won every game.

That night Joseph slept for eight hours solid, untroubled by the morbid, drugged dreams of those last months, and he woke fully rested. He lay and listened to the chickens squawking and to house martins scurrying. He yawned and stretched slowly, his knotty old muscles elastic again, and he relished their pleasure.

As he got dressed he saw his older grandson, John, who always came home late and left early, drive off to work, in Exeter. Joseph went downstairs. The kitchen was empty. He heard the tractor ignition and stepped outside; he called but Mike didn't turn around, as the tractor coughed and rattled into the lane. He came back in and called his daughter, but there was no reply, so he made himself a mug of strong tea and wondered whether there was any secret to making toast. And he assumed there must be because he burned it, but he ate it anyway and enjoyed the taste of charcoaled bread

beneath the butter and home-made, thick-rind marma-
lade. Then he took his cap and went outside.

He knew he'd died because he felt so light and so at
ease. It occurred to him that that evening he should
challenge Mike to an arm-wrestle, and he laughed out
loud at the idea. He tried to look at the sun and it made
his eyes water.

He walked through the lower fields. The wheat was
high and brittle. He bit some grains and let the dry
nutty flavour linger on his tongue and he wondered
who first discovered how to make flour, and then bread.
He entered the pasture where the dairy herd was grazing and passed among his Friesian cows, patting their
flanks. He rolled up his sleeves and held out his arms,
and the braver among them licked his skin for its salt
with their rough wet tongues, though still like all the
others eyeing him with their dull expression of fear
and reproach. He wondered whether they forgave him
for his life's labour of exploitation and butchery, and
he understood how much he loved this farm, these
animals, this rich and crooked valley.

Joseph walked into the village. As he began climbing Broad Lane he realised he'd left his walking stick
behind, but he also realised that he didn't need it: he
was striding forward, with his bow-legs and his slightly

in-turned toes; his tendons and sinews and leathery veins felt invincible, and he wiped the healthy sweat from his face without pausing. For the first time in he didn't know how long he thought of his wife, whom he once used to walk to Doddiscombsleigh to then court during long walks in Haldon Forest, where, while the Second World War raged far away from them, they made urgent love in the shadows of the pines on a scratchy bed of cones and needles, dry twigs crackling as they moved. But he found that, in truth, he was thinking less of her than of himself – walking, so much walking in his life; he could carry on walking now and he needn't ever stop he felt so strong, he felt he could walk the length of the valley and back again.

Joseph looked around as he walked, peering over hedges and through gates, but there wasn't a soul around. When he got up to the phone box he thought he saw a child running along the lane in the distance, but he wasn't sure. He sat down on the bench at the top of the Brown. The improvised goalposts stood quiet and forlorn. An absurd television image leapt perfectly remembered out of his memory, of the majestic black French defender Marius Trésor lunging into a breathtakingly insane tackle during the 1982 World Cup semi-final.

Joseph felt some tiny drops of rain fall on his hands. He looked up and the sky was a clear, unblemished blue. He wondered whether they were the prickles of pins and needles and he lifted his hands and shook them, and ran them down over his face. The world was silent and empty. He knew he'd died three days earlier at three o'clock in the afternoon, and he leaned forward with his head in his hands and wept.

When he heard the church bell tolling he wiped his eyes with his damp sweaty handkerchief, which made his eyes sting, and walked up past the almshouses and then the village hall where he'd once gone to school, and he walked through the lychgate into the graveyard. Twenty yards away they were lowering the coffin into the ground and the rector read from his Bible but Joseph couldn't hear him. Then the rector, still reading, picked up a handful of soil and threw it into the grave and that he did hear, faintly, granules scattering across the lid of the coffin.

He knew everyone there: Granny Sims, for twenty years his fellow churchwarden; Douglas Westcott; old Freemantle and his fragmented family; Martin the retired hedge-layer; Elsie and Stuart from the shop.

As to his own family, in front of the various cousins and nieces and nephews, John held his mother Joan's arm, while Mike looked like he ought to sit down, because he was leaning a little too much of his weight against his girlfriend, whose name Joseph never could remember.

He looked across the graveyard at them and for the first time since his death Joseph felt a sudden upsurge of anger. It swelled inside him, pure and physical: a rage of bile, while his heart pumped hot blood through his veins. Volcanic anger. Anger so strong he thought he might burst.

He closed his eyes, clenched his fists and gritted his teeth. And then he shouted out, 'Why did you not show me this world before, you bastard?' as he lifted his eyes to the wide blue sky, and felt himself light and rising.

Harvest

She dug all through that spring. She dug the earth. After the children had gone to bed Sarah stepped out of the back door, and in the chill evenings she turned the earth over. The vegetable plot had been abandoned years before. If a person was going to sow in the spring they should have dug and manured back in early winter, she knew that much. Added fertiliser, lime maybe, according to a gift-wrapped *A–Z of Gardening* she found in a drawer clearing out their married quarters. Had he intended it for her? She would never know.

The compulsion to dig into the earth, though, seized hold of her, and she obeyed it. Digging deep, stooping, pulling the fleshy roots of dogged perennial weeds. Clay and silt and sand churned together ten thousand years earlier into this rich topsoil gave off a dank, archaic odour she inhaled, and couldn't hold fast enough. Standing up, backache made her groan, a pain she came to relish.

Her tears were lost in the dark soil. She broke open clods of mud with her hands. Worms emerged as if she had liberated them, but this was their terrain, they had the run of it. What now took place was a collaboration: worms broke down matter with their digestion, Sarah tilled it laboriously, until damp earth gave way; crumbled in her grasp. It clung to her skin, silting under her nails, highlighting the lines and cracks on her fingers, ageing her.

The night before David joined his battalion she had woken, disturbed by his mind sawing beside her in the silence.

'What are you thinking?' she asked; in the dim seconds waiting for his answer knew she wanted only to hear of his love for her; and how their children – that genetic duet of theirs – had become the only heroic legacy he needed.

'The peaceniks,' he said.

'What?'

'The human shields, already there, in position. Before us! Already shipped out, and cosied up with their hosts. Welcome guests, don't you think?'

He was alert. Lying on his back, fiercely awake. Artificial light outlined the curtains, seeped weakly into their bedroom; the shape of wardrobe, dresser, emerged vaguely from the mirk. There were hours yet before the undesired dawn, and no more profit to be had from them, she figured, than in sleeping.

'They don't support you, those peaceniks,' she said. 'They don't support us.'

'I wasn't thinking that,' he said.

'They have no idea, do they, those people? Of what, of who, guarantees their freedom.'

He said, 'That's not what was in my mind. I was thinking of the tough guys left back home here.'

'Which guys?'

'The hardballs. You know? Who sound off in the bars and the dinner parties. And write columns in your free newspapers arguing the case for war. Hard-boiled truth-tellers making mock apologies for seeing the world as it really is. Tough enough to commit their views to print. In bold black and white. And take payment. I mean, look, they've got mortgages to pay, haven't they? Kids to get through school.'

She knew him in this tensile mood: he was off now. The calmest of men, her husband; but occasionally something riled him and he would worry away at it, gnawing it through till it was all chewed up. His eyes gleamed in the dark; she could feel his muscled body fraught.

'The tough guys,' he repeated. 'Who believe more than we do, Sarah, in the accuracy – the righteousness – of our heat-seeking missiles. Our smart weapons. Our sci-fi. The big boys back home, you know? With their faith in our precision bombing. Oh, they regret that there may be collateral damage, there always is in war, but *less* this time, you see. Our expertise, our compassion, will ensure it.'

'Yes,' she murmured tiredly, wondering whether in bedrooms dotted all around the country other partners lay with their men and women grinding out resentment on the eve of departure. 'Yes, David. Those guys support you.'

'No, no, they're the ones, Sarah, don't you see, who should have gone? Who should be there. Well away from target areas, of course. I'm not being funny. Far from army bases and anti-aircraft batteries. But it's the wrong way round, for Christ's sake. Those who believe should be there. Not the protestors. The *champions* of war. Put up in some quiet residential quarter of the capital. Sitting on an upturned oil drum in ... a busy marketplace. Camped out in the desert surrounded by ... sheep, sand, blue sky.'

What did he mean, exactly? Should she ask? Did he want her to ask? A spouse should know the answer to such questions, at such a moment.

'Why?' she ventured.

'Why? Why? Just ... I don't know. Just to feel how the earth shudders when our missiles land.'

She put her arm across his chest, squeezed his upper arm. Sarah felt herself tremble against David's ribs, knowing there was nothing she could do to keep him here.

His battalion flew to the Gulf, where they played little part in the campaign but were kept on for the peace. He and the men in his platoon were manning a roadblock, according to the visiting officer, who with the garrison padre came marching through the patch in formal uniform to break the news of his death. There was no body. There were body parts, as Sarah discovered later when she asked to see him, seeking closure.

There were parts of a number of bodies. The bomber had eased his car, packed with three hundred pounds of home-made explosive, into the clamorous throng of people. Forensics had analysed the scene and it was believed that all victims had been accounted for.

Seven people were killed; eleven injured, more or less severely. Native passers-by as well as foreign nationals in uniform. A child of three, a girl, was blown apart – was she grateful, Sarah wondered, for this unasked-for martyrdom?

And her husband, infidel soldier, who according to witnesses was leaning towards the car when, at eleven thirteen a.m. local time, the bomber triggered the explosion.

'Where is he?' the children demanded.

'I don't know,' she said. 'Nowhere.' What could she tell them?

'You must know,' the boy persevered.

'He's dissolved into the universe,' she said. 'I'm sorry. He lived – we loved him, he loved us – he died. Death means oblivion. Your father no longer exists – except in us.'

'But his soul,' the girl insisted. 'I don't care what *you* think: *I* believe in life after death.'

'Why don't we say …?' the boy offered, twisting his mouth as he thought, the way his father had. 'Let's just say, he's in another dimension.'

'Yes,' the girl agreed. 'All right. And he can see us.'

The boy frowned. 'I think that's true.'

Her vegetable plot was cleared of all enemies: nettle, bindweed, dock. Couch grass, creeping thistle and a hundred unidentified species of weed. Swept clean, pristine, a deep and ample bed.

Seed potatoes had sat in egg boxes on the windowsill of the gloomy living room, and sprouted. She marked out rows with taut string, cleared drills with a trowel and solemnly offered the vegetables to their places in the soil.

She followed them with broad beans: when he saw those large seeds, her son demanded to sow them, and did so slowly, measuring each eight exact inches between them, his tongue working in concentration. Sarah wondered whether his father had done that as a boy. A boy from a fairy tale, with a magic beanstalk to a land above the blue sky.

She sowed carrots and broccoli, beetroot and courgette. Her daughter watched, unimpressed by her mother's Passion, until in the first week of June she joined her to help sow the seeds of wrinkled garden peas.

'They're so old,' the girl said. 'They're like pea grandparents, aren't they?'

'They are,' Sarah agreed.

They raked the soil flat.

'Do you think he's still there, Mum?'

'Where? In that other dimension, do you mean?'

'Yes. His soul. Would he stay there, or would he move around? I've been thinking about it.'

'What do you reckon?'

'I don't think he would stay in the same place, Mum,' she said. 'Forever. But will he come nearer, or move further away?'

Was that really it? Sarah wondered. The end of it. How could that possibly be, that a solid man, wide feet planted four-square on the earth, the big man in whose body she had sheltered, the reticent lover who adored her, could in one shattering moment have all conscious-ness erased?

Become a memory, fading.

It seemed monumentally unfair to be so bereaved. Her man had gone from the modern world to be murdered in an ancient one, leaving her to grieve with-out the comfort of an old faith. An infuriating injustice.

And with this further maternal dilemma: what consolation could a mother offer her children beyond that which she finds for herself?

'Where is he?' her daughter demanded. It was such a simple question. The simple, unconsoling answer was truthful and insufficient.

How often had he touched her? Had she caressed every pinch of his skin? How many skins had he shed in the years they'd been together? How many cells of his body, his soul, had rubbed off on her?

It was a Thursday afternoon at the beginning of July that she lifted their first early potatoes. The prongs of her fork speared easily through the soil. She levered the fork back towards her. The flowered stem of the plant rose and she knelt down, plunged her hands into the earth and brought up a clutch of smooth white tubers, none larger than a hen's egg. They snagged on the spindly roots of the original, a rotting old seed potato she'd planted barely two months earlier, now shrivelling from its improbable parentage.

Had she carried him on her hands, and planted him here too, in this soil deposited epochs past? Were there traces of his DNA, then, drawn back up from the mud in the vegetables' substantiation? To nourish this coming evening herself and their children?

Sarah bowed to the earth, ache in her back and in her belly. She fell towards the soil, to the carbon of plants and animals, to the infinite remnants of all the people burned and buried before them; the gardeners and the farmers, old people who'd died in their sleep, soldiers, martyrs, unborn children. All the random, untraceable DNA transforming itself, communicating unknown signals to the future, in the clay and in the sand.

***

Inside, she rubbed the soil off under the tap and boiled the new potatoes, and she and the children ate them with butter and mint.

'They're delicious, Mummy,' her daughter said. 'They really are.'

Fidelity

The white sheets, and the pillowcases, are freshly laundered. Hung to dry on the line out in the garden, they have brought the optimism of the open air to the bed. He is naked.

Ruth wanders between rooms. Remembering things, chores to be done. Toys are picked up from a floor; small clothes chosen, laid out for the morning. She removes her trousers, hangs them on the towel rail beside the chest of drawers, then remembers something else; roams from one room to another in states of undress. Her still-black hair. He watches his wife from the bed: the tasks, combined with her memory, its lapses and recalls, create an erotic display for him.

In the bathroom her body. Nails clipped, cream applied, hairs pulled; she is in there tending herself, with the calm of a gardener. The toilet flushes. Taps run.

There on her bedside table: half-filled crosswords and sudokus; a digital alarm clock; the mug of water he brought upstairs. Outside, the whoosh of traffic noise on Woodstock Road: the sound of waves approaching, breaking on sand, receding. The sky is a darkening blue. Naked, he waits for her.

The girl, the student, he did not notice at first. Beauty was not enough in itself to distract him. Nor was youth. He wasn't sure. It was only when her intelligence became apparent that he fell.

There were certain points to ram home. *Show, don't tell. Detail. What moves you, really? Use all your senses. Again: detail.*

Then at the same moment, in the fifth or sixth week, almost every member of the class produced similar, competent, touching stories. Often they involved grandparents. The difference between the talented one or two and the rest, evident from day one, became blurred. Only the really obtuse or confused student fell back, marooned, unaware of being so: one short story set during the English Civil War, the death of a Roundhead volunteer. *His life passed in front of his eyes like a film.*

Strange, though, how he could grade her, her work, with dispassion. If there was any shift of perspective he could not detect it. He was proud of himself for this.

A new term, a new year, will start soon.

Ruth arrives in time at this space, five feet wide, six and a half feet long, their home within their home. He pulls her to him and he tells her with his voice and with his body that he needs her, wants her, must have her. He makes his bodily strength apparent, his assertion the reassurance she requires that she is wanted.

She is tired. He kisses her. Strokes skin; caresses flesh. Feels in Ruth's kiss the decision taken, to proceed.

She was gifted, the student, that was certain. He thought of the dross he'd produced at her age, and shuddered. Perhaps her ability stirred a vampiric element to his desire: he imagined vanquishing her, taking unto himself her power as right of conquest.

Her rapture a surrender, of her talent to him.

The opposite was also true: she would squeeze him dry, suck the last dregs of his talent from him, render him obsolete. Succeed him.

Talent was important, it was the only thing that mattered. Rare and precious. Actually, it was two a penny; weren't there any number of talented writers, most of whom failed to flourish? Talent was worthless without persistence. If she lacked either will or stamina to carry on through inevitable rejection, and periods of dullness, and despair, then her talent would come to be seen as misleading: something others had wrongfully encouraged, or an inexplicable self-deception.

Ruth's September tan. The pale soft areas of her body neglected, uninvited, but private, theirs alone now.

She will shower in the morning. The smell now and the taste of her. She brings her lived-in body to him. The remnants of her day, its exertions, are in the crevices, the folds, of her skin.

The student had wide shoulders. Pert nose, hooded eyes, suspicious, shy, arrogant. Self-absorbed in a way that talent, intelligence, youth assumed forgiveness of. She rarely smiled, even or especially at other people's wit. Gave little of herself away. Gave little. She was reserved, aloof, inscrutable. So young; age might do anything to her, it was impossible to speculate.

Because of his attention, his desire, aching towards her, he could not help but see her gestures, her attention, as directed towards him. A provocative languidity.

He wants to make it new. He tries with inarticulate tongue, with clumsy, inadequate hands, to fashion a sentence addressed to his wife alone, a sentence that will make her senses bloom. It is beyond him. He both cleaves to and abandons her. She is on her own. When at last Ruth tenses, groaning, pushing him away, she is transformed. Muscles asserting themselves, rippling up through soft flesh to the surface.

The girl's wide shoulders he came to see as exemplary. Wide-shouldered women had style, didn't they?

Class. Swagger, almost. She could have stepped out of a photograph of the Côte d'Azur in 1925, bronzed, newly married, smoking on the esplanade. Young and hard. The world was hers for the taking.

He rises up Ruth's body, they kiss. Her face is flushed. He delivers the taste of her from his mouth to hers, his lips to her tongue, as if she desired to know the taste but needed him to circumvent her ambivalence.

His desire quickens.

They become one now. Again. The familiarity of their fit. The bedstead complains. Ruth's eyes are closed, she could be anywhere, he doesn't know. He bends towards her neck, grasps her head, hides.

The girl was naked, but still she was proud. She knew, somehow, that she possessed riches which had been his, but were leaching from him. Time was dragging him, spiralling his energies away from her. He knelt, clutched her legs, pulled her down, and she fell, laughing, laughing at him.

Ruth opens her eyes, they are narrowed, does she see him?

He is hers. The world is irresistible. Barriers crumble. He is gasping.

He rolls off her. They lie asunder. His lungs crave equilibrium; silence. He hears their son, in his room across the landing, yawn in his sleep.

What did he hope for from his students? That they would become more involved readers, of course. That they would enjoy writing as they might enjoy playing the piano. They all expected publication, though; money, fame. She too, yes of course, why not?

Clothes pulled back on. Outside, he rolls a cigarette. The nights are not yet cold. The sun has set behind Wytham Woods and their garden is bathed in a yellow light. He has poured into this glass what was left in the bottle, the last of the wine brought back from Cahors. The long night drive to the ferry.

On the crossing over, on the way to their holiday, he had taken their daughter out on deck: sea-bright sun, foam and spray and salt air, dazzle and power, the huge boat throbbing through deep water. What would her imagination make of this? he wondered. Would it provide her with material for the rest of her life? She spent the first days in the Dordogne saying, 'When are we going on the ship, Daddy? I want to go on the ship.'

The light in the garden fades, from yellow to grey. There is sound. No, not sound, movement. Is there? Perhaps not. He smokes, an occasional cigarette. She smoked on the Côte d'Azur. No, on the bench outside the college chapel, the student, alone, aloof from her fellows, he glimpsed her back in June. Talent and loneliness. She sent out an invitation, spun from her pen into the air, offering him nothing, inviting him only to see her and be glad and make of her what he might.

He realises suddenly that the movement is on the lawn, a few feet away from him. A small animal, it's a hedgehog. What is it doing? Strange motion. Is it sweeping the grass, looking for insects? What a shame his son and daughter are asleep. His mother once woke his sisters and himself and took them to watch badgers, in a sett in the woods behind their home. Recollected wonder. Yes! He will go and wake the boy now. He stands. The hedgehog scuttles off into the gloom.

Should you write what you know? they asked.

What's important is what you know while you're writing. He told them the story of Maxim Gorky, whose scream brought his wife rushing to his study. She found him on the floor, clutching his stomach. He'd been writing a story in which a man stabs his wife.

Love all your characters, he said. He saw their scepticism. *Identify with them, every one.*

He admitted once telling Louis de Bernières how he must have enjoyed the research into hallucinogenic drugs for his South American trilogy. De Bernières looked at him with pity, perhaps contempt, and said that we were blessed with imagination, were we not?

'I'll bet he did,' the girl said, unsmiling. 'Never believe a writer.'

Be true to yourself, he said to them, opening his hands. *Your way of seeing.*

'Be true.' How easy it was to say.

He spits out toothpaste. It is red with blood. No, not blood, wine. He stares at himself. He thinks he has come up now, on to some plateau of contentment. A place that is and will continue to be ridiculous. He will reach the far side of this plateau if he is lucky, that is all. There will be no more progress, only children, growing.

He lowers the seat and the lid of the toilet before flushing it in the silent house. Closes the bathroom door.

His daughter is sleeping. She looks exhausted, as if sleep itself is tiring her. Floating, dreams swell in her vacant head, the ocean in all its surging immensity surrounds her.

His wife too seems to be asleep now. She has left his light on. He slides into bed. As he settles his body on the firm mattress, Ruth murmurs. He stretches out an arm, and switches off the light.

Invisible Children

'You need to tell her, soldier,' Bill said. We lay on a slope, surrounded by hundreds of people. It was like some vast nocturnal picnic, except for the music thumping out of the big tents. Sara and the others were down there, still dancing. The night was black above our heads. Lights fizzled and splashed up the hill.

I said, 'I'll never tell her. I shouldn't have told you.'

Bill smiled. 'I always knew,' he said.

We'd been dancing three solid hours. The racket of beats reverberated around our skulls. I can't think how loudly we must have been speaking in order to hear each other.

'Some things are better left unsaid.' I tried to roll a cigarette. The drug was making my fingers tremble. Bill shook his head and lay back on the hard earth. I said, 'People need space.' I licked the paper, rolled it more or less tight, lit the cigarette. The drug made it feel like you'd chosen to inhale something more complex, more substantial, than smoke. I exhaled. 'It's good for friends,' I said, 'when there's something unspoken between them.'

Guy came out of the tent and, dressed in his pork pie hat and shirt and tie, headed up the slope towards us, weaving to the beat through pairs and clusters of people. When he reached us he stood, gazing beyond us, dancing on the spot, unable to shake all of the rhythm out of his limbs.

'Biblical,' Guy pronounced at length, nodding his head. Then he flourished two fruit bars and passed us one each.

I'd ummed and ahed about coming for weeks. My wife, Jen, teased my indecision. 'Go,' she said. 'Get it out of your head.'

Bill and the others left London on Friday morning, to get there in good time. I drove down from Oxford after work, alone, listening to Bach's *Art of Fugue* on the car cassette player, and I called Bill as I walked in across the fields of parked cars. Early evening sunshine reflected off bonnets and windscreens. Bill met me at the security barrier, an official beckoned me through. The ticket was scanned by a barcode reader. The official attached a band to my wrist, on which were printed the words *12 Stages. 3 Days. Open Air. Belter.*

From where we lay on the slope we could see four or five of the big tents. Some cute new sound system in operation kept the sound fields from overlapping. We could only hear the psy-trance we'd been dancing to. Breakbeats were over there, a chill tent beyond.

'When are you going to tell her?' Bill asked.

I took a last drag of my cigarette, and stubbed it out on the hard ground. 'Why would I tell her now?' I said. 'It's ten years too late. It wouldn't do anyone any good.'

'It's never too late,' he said.

I didn't want to talk. The drug was in me and I was ready to dance again. 'He's my oldest friend,' I said. 'I knew him before I knew you. I'd have to tell him first, and what good would that do?'

'Speak of the devil,' said Bill.

Cal sauntered up the slope, saluting when he saw us. He was holding Sara's hand; she was a pace behind him. A stranger could enjoy interpreting their relationship from observing the way they ascended the cracked earth. Was he dragging her up the hill or forcing her back behind him? Was she being towed reluctantly away from the music, or grateful to be given some assistance?

Cal was tall, he'd always been the one to follow through the crowd or regain your bearings by if you'd strayed, and he was well built, but soft. You could still tell how handsome he used to be. Cal possessed the assurance of a man who informs company executives what they're doing wrong in the way they run their operations, and how to put it right, a privilege for which they pay him charming amounts of money. He'd received approval from birth, had Cal Simmons. He expected it. I doubted whether anyone had ever taken a pop at him, and whenever I imagined doing so myself I was sure he'd fail to see it coming. If I could just land one good swing on his lantern jaw that'd be all it would take, I suspected: Cal's knees would buckle, and he had a lovely long way to fall.

It was odd, really, this fantasy only occurred to me when I was actually in Cal's benevolent presence, so that I'd not entertained it in years, but seeing the two of them again brought it right back. They sat in front of us. Cal let out a long, breathy sigh. 'Jesus, it's going off, isn't it?' he said.

'Who's playing?' Bill asked him.

'Give me that map, will you, babe?'

Sara passed Cal a piece of thin cardboard which he unfolded and held in front of him. I gave him my lighter. He lit it, and as he raised it up I imagined others across the hill copying him, holding their lighters up too, the way those fans at rock gigs used to do.

'Liquid Elf,' Cal declared.

I offered Sara my water bottle. She took a glug. What's sad, I thought, is the way you lose touch by degrees. It wasn't easy for Sara when we had our first child; she and Cal had been trying awhile, Jen made no effort at all; and then we moved out of London. 'How are you doing?' I asked her.

Sara kind of blinked in that self-deprecating way she always had, and smiled. 'I'm a bit spangled,' she said.

Sara's beauty was something people tended not to notice at first. She didn't turn men's heads. She hid behind large framed spectacles, the brown hair which fell either side of her face and her posture: Sara hunched her shoulders and hid herself from strangers. You had to get to know her to be able to see her. And then you thought about what you had to do about what you saw. I thought I had, long ago.

'You've put on weight,' she said. 'Family life must suit you.'

'I eat the children's leftover food,' I said. 'Fathers do.' I was lying on my side.

'Can I roll one?' Sara asked, seeing the tobacco on the ground behind me. She leaned over my torso. 'I don't want to smoke it,' she said, wincing, as if I had suggested she should. 'I just want to roll one for you.' It took her awhile, draped lazily across me, deep in concentration, her tactility like a child's.

We rested on our elbows, watching the multitude below milling to and fro between music tents and food counters, and the stalls selling fluoro clothes or drug paraphernalia, or an odd one I'd noticed, doing no business, which featured nothing but multicoloured wellies. I could just make out a fire-eater on the circus stage; earlier, we'd watched a juggler there, and girls gyrating hula hoops. On the open ground the crowds passed beneath banners, streamers, statues shaped like undreamed-of mushrooms. Some were lit from within, others illuminated by the lights spilling and flashing from the marquees.

***

I felt like I'd come out of retirement. All-night parties, never mind whole weekends, were incompatible with fatherhood. Some things had changed since the days we drove to Wales for free parties deep in forest plantations. Instead of wandering around lost, as we often seemed to do, now people texted each other on their mobile phones as they trudged about. And when they danced everybody seemed to face the stage, as if a person putting on records — or rather operating a computer — was some kind of spectacle. No one else appeared to be troubled by anything sinister in this, nor by the gluttonous excess of a dozen stages.

The music, to my surprise, sounded pretty much the same. What had erupted in the musical landscape fifteen years earlier, unlike anything in the history of man-made sound, seemed to have then evolved no further.

'Oh, man,' said Cal. 'I love these beats.'

He'd stood up and was dancing, two emphatic treads on one foot, then two on the other, then back to the first, while his torso jerked to the 4/4 beat and his hands played an invisible drum. It was the same movement, whatever track was playing. As he pounded away, rotating gradually in a clockwise direction, Cal gazed into the far distance through his wire-rimmed glasses, so that it was impossible to tell whether he was addressing anyone in particular: 'I think I'll go and piss against that tree,' he said, though he didn't move. It seemed like he was letting us know of some future manoeuvre he was planning to carry out.

Guy reappeared with bottles of mineral water, which he passed around. 'I've been talking to people.' He smiled, like he had a joke to tell us. 'Severe weather warnings.' He grinned, as if these words were the punchline.

'You're kidding,' Bill said, spreading his hands. 'Can you imagine a more perfect summer night?'

'Flood warnings are being issued by the Met Office. The AA and the RAC are warning drivers to stay off the roads.'

'Good job we're not planning any road trips,' said Cal, and everyone laughed.

We headed down the slope. The others were all from the old crowd, 'the childless survivors' as my wife referred to them. Bill had taken more drugs, slept less and danced for longer than the rest of us put together. I had fond memories of him holding dazed audiences in thrall in forest clearings, spouting inspired gibberish about mushroom cults in the Middle Kingdoms or the connection between deep geological activity and crop circles in England's wheat fields. Bill had charisma, and no ambition. Here he was, in all his regalia: a wizard's hat and cape, covered in silver stars, and a wand which he held like a baton, conducting his friends and the wider crowd around him.

Guy, who never took drugs, was bouncing up and down beside him, pausing at regular intervals to replenish his energy with fruit juice and vitamins. We danced, the group of us together, the music hard and sustained, the beats a perfect balance of predictable and unexpected, our bodies taking us on a journey through layers of sound.

When, at four in the morning, the last of the stages shut down for the night, we headed across a field towards our tents. Stars sparkled in the black sky, aware of the enchantment below.

In recent years I'd become accustomed to campsites around Britain: our children adored the unfamiliar deprivations of life under canvas, as their mother had before them.

Bill and the gang had corralled me a place amidst their laager barely large enough for my cheap one-man tent, which I'd bought the day before, and it was odd putting it up, pulling the guy ropes into narrow alleys between other tents in order to peg them. 'I'm not saying these tents are close together,' I said. 'I just hope none of you snore.'

Apart from Guy, whose shelter was a white gazebo wrapped around with blue plastic fly-sheets, they were all small, globular one- or two-person tents, stuck like anemones to the surface of the sun-scorched earth. Here and there tents glowed from within. We shared hugs goodnight outside the gazebo.

'Glad you came, soldier?' Bill asked me.

'Oh, yes,' I said, squeezing his solid frame. 'I am so glad. So, so glad.' How had I forsaken this rapture, why denied it myself in return for the more bland, profound pleasure of parenthood? Family life could perfectly well accommodate an occasional foray into ecstasy. Who or what had planted this self-denying seed in my personality? The fading religious ethics of my parents, or a caution within my own character?

Sara, tall and slender, hugged gently, though for longer than she needed to. Her small, high breasts; her belly; her vacant womb. She'd been dancing for hours, her neck smelled sharp and sweet. I'd been wishing to kiss Sara Simmons for thirteen years. Did she know that? I guessed she knew. But maybe she didn't.

No sooner had I laid down my head than the rain began falling, tapping softly at first on the roofs of the tents. My groggy brain reconfigured the sound as purposeful percussion, as if the music in the glade had inspired the heavens, nature responding with a delicate tattoo. Picturing first Jen and then the children each asleep in bed at home, I began myself to fall asleep, to the rhythm of the rain gradually intensifying in volume and complexity.

It was still dark when I awoke. For a moment I thought we were under bombardment. The rain hammered on the plastic roof so hard you could no longer differentiate separate raindrops in what was a constant roar. I doubted very much whether I'd paid enough money for the tent. The thunder alone, rumbling angrily around the valley before exploding above, would probably blast it loose. That was if the lightning didn't strike first: it seemed to bite the ground nearby and then light up the world in horrifying flashes of insanity, in which I could see water coursing all around me, along the channels between our tents.

I needed to pee. I'd brought an empty five-litre plastic water bottle, as Bill advised. He'd also recommended I bring earplugs and a travel shade. I filled my ears and covered my eyes, and went back to sleep.

We began to stir from our positions around noon, heads emerging warily from tent flaps. The rain had abated somewhat, scaled back to a grudging drizzle.

'Looks like the worst is over,' said Guy, standing in the same outfit as yesterday, minus his trousers: hat, shirt, tie and boxer shorts.

'Maybe it's only a respite,' I said.

I stood and watched people trooping towards the glade or in other directions, to toilets and showers, or off to their vehicles to stock up on supplies, their feet slipping and sinking in the soft, wet grass.

'I'm off on a coffee and croissant run,' said Guy. 'Anyone got any orders?'

We congregated in Guy's gazebo. You could almost stand up in it, except that two of the legs had buckled and the whole thing tilted, which probably helped drain off the rain. It was falling hard again, beating down upon the plastic and the soil. People retreated into their own vacant thoughts.

Bill lay on his back with his eyes closed, and he started spouting some nonsense about the rain cults of certain South American tribes, but he didn't seem to have the heart for it, and after a while lapsed into silence.

Cal entered the gazebo, bending his head. Sara followed him in.

'Anyone ever been to Bhutan?' he asked. No one responded, so Cal sat down, on one of Guy's fold-up chairs, without sharing whatever thought he'd come in with. Sara sat on the blow-up sofa next to me. Her weight made it sink in the middle, pressing us together.

'You okay?' I asked her.

She nodded. 'Some night.' She shook her head. 'Some storm. I mean, scary, but fantastic, no?'

'Yes,' I said.

When, in the afternoon, the rain suddenly stopped, we made a sortie. Patches of blue bloomed in the grey sky and the sun shone bright. We joined the throng, plodding through mud. You had to watch where you walked, you didn't know with each step whether your foot was going to slide from under you or get stuck.

'This raw smell,' said Sara, treading stealthily. 'Does it mean there's shit mixed up in this?'

No one else answered, so I said, 'It's just the smell of churned-up mud.'

'So says our agricultural expert from Oxford,' said Cal. People chuckled without looking up.

By the time we got to the wellies stall, a big sign declared SOLD OUT.

We ate burritos and fajitas. Guy insisted on standing a round of smoothies. Bill blagged a bunch of plastic bags from a music stall. They came in different colours, and I chose a bright yellow pair: we removed our trainers, stepped into the bags, put back on our shoes and tied the bags as high up our legs as possible.

Above us the sun was swallowed up again and the clouds spat upon the mob below. Although there were signs here and there of defiant fancy dress – a young man in Edwardian monocle and gaiters; a space girl with purple hair – no one could deny that the mood had changed. Replacing the blissed-out ease of the day before, you could tell from their demeanour that people were preparing to call upon reserves of fortitude and stamina it had not occurred to them they'd need in order to make this festival hum.

We lumbered after Cal through the thick and sticky mud, to a stage in front of which a hundred people, feet planted in the sludge, twisted and shimmied. Dancing from the knees up.

Bill lit his chillum and passed it round. Cal danced in his customary manner, stomping two beats on each foot, tamping down the clay. Guy swayed beside him. Up on the stage, either side of the DJ's console, two women in luminous orange and yellow tight-fitting outfits, with long yellow and orange hair extensions, cavorted with unrestrained energy, attempting to enliven the crowd. The thud of the music was meant to make the ground bounce, and bodies rise off it, but the beat sank in the mud.

My eyes met Sara's, and we smiled at each other. It was as if we knew what each other thought, and were smiling at the same things, the very same absurdities.

When I glanced up through the netting above us and saw how coal-black the sky was, I actually yelped a warning. It was too late. Raindrops fell like pellets machine-gunned from the clouds and splattered on our heads, ricocheted off surfaces, exploded on open ground.

Our company staggered to the beer tent. Others followed and shouldered their way through, till we found ourselves hemmed in. The rain fell more and more heavily, so thick that all you could see outside was the ground, bubbling and seething. Occasionally a figure emerged, utterly drenched, tottering towards our haven, pushing his or her way in. The crush, the warm rain, the heat of such proximity brought forth the odours of people's clothes and bodies. Guy alone was somehow able to move, squeezing through to the bar and back again with pint-sized plastic beakers of cold beer he passed around, grinning behind his shades as if already relishing what memories this fiasco would furnish him with, to reminisce the long year through.

'You know what they're calling this?' he asked.

No one asked Guy who 'they' might be, nor what 'this' was. Instead, reflected in the insectile mirrors of Guy's sunglasses, we waited in that malodorous crush for him to tell us what they called it.

'An extreme rainfall event.'

The rain paused after a while and we ventured back outside. The ground was liquid mud now, slippery, easier to dance in though more hazardous. We gave it a go. A big naked man, spray-painted bronze, darted in and out of the crowd, his stub of a penis stuck on to his bollocks like a piece of clay. Out on her own a pretty, wild-eyed girl was flailing, barefoot, in the quagmire.

When the rain came again we headed back across the open site towards our tents, water flowing down the slope in widening streams. We passed an audience gathered, jeering, around a pair of lads wrestling in slime. They were either friends or incompetent enemies.

We slithered through the ooze. Cal lurched in front. Bill slid as if his shoes were skis, turning the precarious passage into sport. Sara lost her footing and flung out her arms, but I was there, and caught her.

People stood about like stragglers, left behind. Celtic men, woad-painted, with shaven heads and runic tattoos. Their Boadicea women. Bedraggled girls in bikini tops and mud-spattered leggings, some with wings on their backs. Nature – vegetal, swampy – had dragged them to the ground, angels in the mud.

'Have you told her yet?'

'Will you keep your voice down?' I was lying in my sleeping bag. Bill lay beside me. We stared at the low ceiling of my cheap tent. With every second it withstood the barrage, I appreciated what a bargain it had been. Guy had announced that he was retiring to his gazebo for a late siesta, and we'd all elected to do the same.

'If you have feelings for someone, you should tell them,' he said. 'However complicated that makes things.'

'I didn't know they'd be here,' I said.

'I thought you knew.'

'You didn't tell me.'

'I would have,' Bill assured me. He raised himself on to all fours. 'I'm off to get some shut-eye for tonight. There's so many great acts on I don't know which tent to go to. The big night.'

Bill was a positive force in my life. I was so grateful he hadn't given up on me. 'I thought tomorrow was the big night,' I said. 'The climax of the festival.'

'It is, yeh,' Bill agreed, as he clambered towards the tent flap. 'But that's tomorrow. And tonight, soldier, is tonight.'

After Bill had left I rolled and smoked a cigarette, and peed into the water bottle, and then I lay down waiting to doze off, the sound of the rain soporific even as it pounded on the roof of the tent and roared away outside.

When I woke, an hour or two later, the rain seemed even louder. After a while, I realised that there were other noises, too. Human ones. I couldn't make out what they were saying, but something – inflection, perhaps, or emphasis – seemed to suggest that one of them was Cal's. I can't be any more specific than that. For a horrible moment it occurred to me that it was the sound of sex, and I reached for the earplugs, but then I heard Sara's voice: 'I don't *care*.'

I began, then, as I lay there, to concentrate, focusing my attention in the direction of the tent next to mine. Odd phrases came through to me. 'Toilets are rank,' Sara said. 'Overflowing.' I suppose the truth is, they spoke louder as they argued.

'How can you even consider it?' Cal said. 'No. No way. We're all in this together.' And then again, after some mumbled sentence I couldn't decipher, 'We're a group. A team.'

I realised quite suddenly that I could hear what they were saying not because of unique aural powers I'd turned out to possess, but because they were no longer in their tent but standing outside it, in the gulley between theirs and mine. What Sara was saying, at that moment, was, 'All I want to do is leave. Is it so much to ask?'

I opened my tent flap. I couldn't see them, around the side, so I crawled right out and stood up. Cal and Sara faced each other two or three feet apart, drenched, the fast-running stream that coursed between the tents breaking around their calves like the pillars of bridges, yelling at each other through the roaring rain.

'I didn't pay all this money for tickets,' Cal told her, 'so we could miss out on the best part.'

'I'd pay as much again,' Sara shouted back at him, 'to get out of here.'

'You didn't pay in the first place,' Cal yelled. 'I did.'

I spoke quite softly, but it was clear that they – and probably the others, too, listening in their tents as I'd been – could hear me.

'I'll take you home.'

They each turned slowly and stared, incredulous, as much at the sight of me, standing there soaked through, as at what I'd said.

'Who the fuck's asking you?' Cal bawled in my direction, but Sara stepped towards me.

There were plenty of other deserters, slithering and stumbling towards the exit, clutching rucksacks and binbags. Many left their tents behind. In the parking fields it was mayhem. Dishevelled knots of people pushed cars, which took off suddenly and careered crazily across greasy patches of grass before slowing to a stop, and sinking into mud.

I drove backwards and forwards a few feet, half-heartedly, aware that we were trapped. The last thing I wanted was to have to go back to the others for help.

Off in the distance a young farmer – perhaps the owner of these pastures – was buzzing about on a tractor, towing people out. When at last he came our way I hailed him and he turned towards us, the big wheels of his vehicle sprightly in the mire, churning the earth up further, making itself ever more indispensable.

The farmer swung the tractor round and reversed along the alley in front of our avenue of cars, twisting in his seat. He came to a stop and called out, 'Twenty quid, buddy.' I nodded, and he jumped down from his cab and came forward carrying the hook of a tow rope, bending as he approached, peering beneath my car.

It felt curiously regal being towed out of the car park behind a tractor. I wanted to wave as we cruised past those still marooned. Here and there in vacant spaces between cars you could see pairs of wellington boots upright in the mud, where their owners, I guess, had simply stepped into their cars and driven away.

The strangest thing was that even as we and others were leaving, so just as many, it seemed, were coming in. Infantry reinforcements plodded in by foot, others were ferried on the bus shuttle to and from the local train station. As we drove slowly through wide, deep puddles along the lane away from the site, other cars full of anxious, excited faces passed us, heading in the opposite direction. We carved our respective ways through the brown water like boats, the lines of our wakes meeting in little shimmies of turbulence in the middle of the road.

I had my headlights on, the windscreen wipers on full. After a mile or two we passed a filling station, and then a shopping centre with a supermarket, a pet emporium, a computer warehouse. We drove past a golf course. Two figures wandered across the rain-drenched fairways. You could see that even if, for a moment, you'd been at the centre of things, all around you life had carried on.

Until now, Sara had said nothing since nodding her assent to me between our tents an hour or two earlier. She was drying her hair with a towel, and then she said, 'I am so grateful.'

'Me too,' I said. 'Believe me.'

'So relieved not to be there any more. I mean, how could it not get much, much worse?'

'They'll have a fine time. You'll see.'

'They'll take a lot more drugs.'

'I just couldn't,' I said.

'Cal won't stop,' Sara said, exasperation and affection coexisting in her voice.

'What you've done,' I said, 'is make time out of nothing.'

I sensed Sara turn towards me. I dared not take my own eyes off the ill-visible road.

'I'll get you back to London,' I continued, 'by … what time is it? … by nine. You'll have the rest of this evening and the whole of tomorrow when you thought you'd be away. No commitments. Nobody knows where you are. No obligations. You can do whatever you want.'

I told her of the time a year or so before when Jen and myself and our children were going away for the weekend. Some family occasion. The children had been sick that week. My wife and I bickered packing the car, the children took it in turns to sulk or whine, we left too late and drove too fast along the road out of town. Jen slowed down, pulled over, switched off the engine. 'We don't need to go,' she said. 'Call. Tell them we're ill. Couldn't we? And just go home.'

We spent the next morning lounging around and then, replenished, had a wonderful weekend, doing things we were usually too busy to do. Even as I told Sara this story, I was unable to explain why I was doing so.

'You're right,' Sara said, nodding, looking ahead. 'It's the same. We can do whatever we want.'

We, I thought, but said nothing. I had the feeling, in the long pause that followed, that the light changed inside the car: as if a spectre of sunshine made it weakly through the rain. The vehicle hurtled forward, but inside it all was utterly still.

Sara eventually turned to me. 'I can't let you go home,' she said. 'Without a hot bath, a meal. Look at you: those ridiculous bags on your feet.' You can hear someone's smile in an alteration of tone. 'A change of clothing. You can wear Cal's.' Sara laughed softly. 'Anything you like.' Her lovely laugh, suggestive of some subtlety beyond the obvious meaning. I'd always had the feeling Cal never quite got it.

We competed for a while over things people could do in London on an unexpectedly free Sunday. Given that I'd left the capital ten years before, it wasn't surprising that Sara came up with more than me. There were hardly any cars on the M4 heading east, into town. The rain swayed lazily over the empty lanes. Yellow headlights flickered across the central reservation.

We drove along the flyover, past the company towers and the office blocks, coming into Chiswick. 'Could you roll me a cigarette?' I asked.

The rain was slackening off, the sky becoming lighter just as this long summer day drew on into evening. I switched off the windscreen wipers. On either side of the road ahead, like a series of blank screens coming to life, the grey windows of the office blocks began to reflect streaks of gold, and glints of silver, breaking through the clouds. I looked in my rear-view mirror and saw a patch of turquoise sky behind us. I hoped that our friends were happy there, dancing in the mud, dancing in the twilight.

***

There was a vacant parking space a few yards along the pavement from Cal and Sara's front door, off Holland Park Avenue. I hauled Sara's stuff out of the boot and carried it up the steps. She found her keys, and unlocked the door.

'Come on, then,' she said, heading into the hallway.

'I won't stay,' I said. Sara turned. 'I'll get on home.'

'But I thought ... ' Sara said. She looked genuinely disappointed, though it's probable I flatter myself to think so. Then she appeared to tremble with swift resolve. 'You think you'll be welcome home like that?' She was right. I was filthy, smelly and still a little spaced out.

Sara smiled at me. At the same impossibilities that I did. I stepped forward and we hugged briefly, fiercely. 'Take care,' she whispered.

'You too,' I said, before retreating to the car.

Driving up the M40 in the dark, I smoked the cigarette Sara had rolled me. The radio said the rain would be heavy again towards morning. It was nearly nine p.m. I wouldn't have been surprised if at this very moment Jen was failing to usher any of our children to bed; in my absence, indulging them. My guess was that she'd be embroiled on the sofa, the little trio in their pyjamas, watching some old video. Suddenly I wanted more than anything to be but a mile away, driving home, about to surprise them. About to squeeze my way into the scrum of my family, my wife and children who would wriggle and object and make room for me somehow, and let me watch the rest of the tape with them, the smallest on my lap, our blood-filled limbs tight packed together. This, more than anything. I rolled down the window and scattered the rest of the tobacco on the damp tarmac, wondering whether I could make it.

Chemistry

Elizabeth Mitchell admired her only son. Twenty-seven years old, he resided at present in Kraków, to which he'd moved from Berlin six months before, when Poland joined the EU. He could speak a little of the language already, he told her in the email; he rented a small house, with a little orchard garden, in a quiet suburb, and so long as he was flexible there was work to be had, a living made. It was tantamount to an invitation to visit – at least Liz took it so, knowing him as she did, and she booked a week's holiday from her job as a receptionist at the doctor's surgery on Beaumont Street.

Andrew's father was less impressed by their son's 'vagabond existence'. 'Waste of an education,' he lamented. 'Of a perfectly good brain.' John was a historian, who'd made his name unearthing the lives of yeomen and peasants from the substratum of recorded history; when working at home he would emerge from his study and blink in surprise at the wife and son and daughter sharing his house, like some earlier Oxford bachelor don caught in a time warp, until he would shake his head and utter, 'How was school today ... Andrew? Sophie?'

John had hardly registered the struggle Andrew underwent to overcome his shyness. The child would look away when spoken to, unable to sustain eye contact even with his mother. In the presence of other people Andrew was uncomfortable, disturbed, on the brink of flight or tears. Blushing, words came awkwardly from his mouth. He was only happy in his own company, in the garden or the house, untroubled inside his head. Through the years at Wolvercote Primary and then Cherwell School Liz witnessed Andrew suffer – slowly interact, make odd friends; come to terms with human beings – as a parent is accorded the pain and privilege of doing. He survived in the hubbub, making the effort every day to do so, for which Liz admired her son enormously.

'Ryanair?'

'EasyJet,' Liz told her daughter. 'Twenty-seven pounds each way. Ridiculous.'

'Plus taxes,' Sophie said.

'I mean ridiculous how cheap it is.'

'Where from? Stansted?'

'Luton.'

'Exactly how,' Sophie demanded, 'are you going to get from Oxford to Luton? Can't see you on the coach,

Mother.' A sneer evident even down the telephone line. 'You'll be getting Daddy to drive you, I presume.'

'Actually, I'm not,' Liz said, her jaw clenching. 'I'm going to take the Fiat, and leave it in the car park.'

'Ha,' said Sophie. 'You see? I bet that's costing you like a hundred quid. Am I right or wrong?'

Liz had spent three hours on the internet the night before, securing the cheapest flight to Kraków, and Sophie was supposed to share her mother's indignation at the insanity of low-cost air travel.

'Cheap flights are a myth,' she said instead. 'Everyone knows of someone else who flew to Rome for fifteen pence. No one's actually done it.' Sophie gave a peremptory chuckle, a snort without humour. 'There's one born every minute.'

When Liz turned the handset off she could feel it slippery in her grasp, could feel her heart pounding. She noticed two envelopes beside the base, addresses in John's spidery scrawl.

'You want these posting?' she called out. The ensuing silence was a lengthy one, but Liz knew to wait, while John's brain assimilated her syllables through the barriers of his concentrating mind.

'Please,' he called back from far away, and Liz was out of the front door. She walked round the corner into Banbury Road, up the short distance to the round-about, and then across North Way at the double set of pelican crossings. The summer evening was warm but overcast, the atmosphere humid with rumour of rain. She removed her cardigan and wrapped it around her waist. Her daughter annoyed her; she annoyed herself. Traffic noise, from the northern bypass and the inter-connecting dual carriageway to the A34, drummed and rumbled in the air, and Liz let it have its peculiar effect upon her: the noise wrapped her mind as if in some coarse but cushioning fibre. She crossed Five Mile Drive and carried on towards the small lake. Tethered to stakes on suburban lawns and floating on the dark grey water were tiny boats, like toys. Her mind became calm, thoughts drifted from it, as she made the loop around Linkside Avenue and back past the lake, and continued the circuit of her walk towards Woodstock Road.

Sophie was two years younger than Andrew. How differ-ent from each other a brace of siblings could be. The girl spoke without thinking, squeaked and squawled, a single-handed disruption of a studious household. She struck up conversations with strangers – the odder the better – on railway station platforms, crowded beaches. Sophie threw herself into everything Andrew shrank away from. She was always running into things; she had no brakes. While Andrew's childhood was a slow, painful negotiation with society, Sophie's was a drama. She fell out with the friends she made too easily. Liz was obliged to listen to other parents and teachers complaining, offering advice.

Brother and sister had little in common. Forced to spend time together Andrew and Sophie rubbed each other the wrong way, bickered, fought. Each seemed to look down upon the other. As far as possible, they avoided one another.

Things grew worse during Sophie's teenage years. She became lost in the large comprehensive which John insisted their children attend. Her disruptions became quieter, bleaker, more often against herself. She fell in with fellow misfits, smoked dope, binged or starved herself. Turned on her own skin. The promiscuity of her childhood friendships transferred easily to shifting boys.

One day John, glancing up from his morning post, blinked and said, 'What on earth is that thing doing in your nose?' He peered over his spectacles. 'This is north Oxford, Sophie, not Papua New Guinea.'

Less than a week later they were milling in the hallway, making ready to leave for their various destinations, when Andrew said, 'Tell her to open her mouth.'

Sophie invited her brother to shut his own, and stormed out of the front door. But soon enough her father saw the stud embedded in her fourteen-year-old tongue. He said nothing.

It was like living, Liz thought, with a saboteur, of Sophie's own life and of those around her; a familiar stranger who regarded residing with her family as a form of house arrest. They were grim years, every crisis a forbidding one, Liz obliged to intervene repeatedly: Sophie saw counsellors, GPs, a psychiatrist; she took medication as an occasional necessity. Liz's every intervention met with hateful resentment. Sophie's GCSEs were retaken and scraped through, A levels too, and a further gap year was spent dossing around Oxford. Sophie finally left for Bournemouth with, as John put it, 'two A levels, one abortion, a psychotic episode and a criminal record for supplying her friends with dried mushrooms. A promising start.'

Liz felt only numb relief. It seemed to her that the store of maternal love she'd been allotted for her daughter had never replenished itself, and was now exhausted. Still, she kept in contact, with cards, phone calls, emails. She welcomed Sophie home – her wayward daughter and the two distant men, father and brother, would have drifted apart, she was sure – but it was duty that made her do so.

Sophie more or less passed her photography degree, and lived here and there along the south coast. Summers she spent on the road and at festivals, with travellers in trucks, an old ambulance, once a horse-drawn caravan. As far as Liz could gather, her daughter performed, rarely the same thing twice: singing, acting, juggling. 'Our all-round entertainer,' John called her. She dropped in on Oxford occasionally. The last time, in March, Liz was struck by lines in her twenty-five-year-old daughter's face; inflicted, she assumed, by the drugs, and by the summer sun and wind. But she was calmer. The chemical volatility of her youth gradually settling itself.

Shortly before six-thirty, after Elizabeth had returned from her walk, as John was mixing the gin and tonics with which they began a Friday evening, he remarked upon the irony of both his children choosing to become, despite the comparative privilege of their upbringing, modern members of the economic underclass he studied.

'I know,' Liz said.

John frowned, as he cut the lemon. 'It's an irony I find harder to enjoy than certain others might.'

'Andrew won't be working in bars and building sites forever.'

John placed the glass on a coaster on the table beside Liz. 'You see great things ahead?' he asked.

'Perhaps,' she said. She would not rise to the bait. 'Perhaps.'

'I look forward to a progress report.'

Liz scrabbled a handful of salted peanuts from the bowl. 'I'll give him your love,' she said.

John surely knew she would, if he ever considered the matter.

Liz gathered fruit in the orchard of the Polish house. Apples, pears, damsons. It was the middle of August. If she used all her weight she could shake the trunk of a tree from which ripe plums fell, sweet and juicy. The weather was hot and sweaty but not unpleasantly so in the shade of the fruit trees. She made the mistake of going barefoot, once, and was stung by a wasp gorging on the fallen fruit: the precise pain took Liz back almost fifty years, to the garden she'd grown up in, an only child, in a north Oxfordshire village.

There were still a few blackcurrants and raspberries on the bushes here, blackberries coming into season. Walnuts green on a wide-spreading tree.

The house, one half of which Andrew rented, was in Bielany, once a village, now an outlying suburb of Kraków, not far from the small airport Liz flew into. Andrew, behind the barrier, held a sign, 'Mrs Mitchell', his lips twisted in that wry, reticent grin of his, disguised a little now by a wispy beard. His embrace, too, was unchanged: awkward, non-committal, but she hugged him to her all the same, till she had the feel of his flesh, and the smell of him again.

He took her sightseeing, things she guessed he wouldn't do, had not done, himself – just as, after all, she did with visitors to Oxford. They took a tour of the centre of Kraków in a fancy horse-drawn wagon. Its wheels were covered in rubber strips. The driver was a paunchy, red-faced drinker, much younger, she realised, than he first appeared. Every now and again he would turn from his seat in front of and above them, point to whichever church they were passing, and announce, 'Saint Peter and Saint Paul. Seventeen century.' His pair of horses ambled calmly along their familiar route. 'Saint Andrew. Thirteen century.'

***

Liz ate fruit from the garden for breakfast, with yoghurt and honey. The restaurants offered wholesome food: meat or fish, potatoes or dumplings. Andrew ordered for her. He didn't look the waiter or waitress in the eye but his accent sounded pretty much like theirs. '*Proposzę pstrag ruszt, ziemniaki i surowke ... Proszę ... Piwo.*'

They chinked glasses.

'Cheers, Mum.'

'I could have sworn,' she said, 'you weren't a beer drinker.'

'I wasn't. Back home. Warm beer tasting like soap. But out here.' He held up the slim glass of brown liquid. 'At the end of a hot summer's day.' Andrew took a cool throatful and swallowed, murmuring his pleasure. Liz had a sense of the small liberations of exile. She asked him what work he had.

'I'm writing,' Andrew said and grinned lopsidedly. His mother used to encourage his school compositions, stories. 'You're a natural observer,' she used to tell him. 'You're a natural writer.' Yes, he observed other people, keenly as an animal; he did it to survive. He shook his head. 'No. It's commercial crap, Mum. With EU membership, organisations need their written material – advertising, PR stuff – in English.'

'You translate?'

'No. Someone else, I mean Poles, translate the content. What I do's polish their English.'

It occurred to Liz that she'd enjoy telling John of Andrew's progression from physical to intellectual work, however modest: proof of her faith in her son. It was the only time she thought of her husband during the holiday.

Andrew worked at night. Liz slept on a divan, made up with ill-fitting sheets and blanket, in the sitting room. She was woken intermittently, by guard dogs tethered in the gardens of the neighbourhood, barking to each other, and by the *cloc* of pears dropping on the tiled roof of the old barn. In the mornings she picked fruit while Andrew slept. There were yellow apples she quartered, cut out the cores: within moments the white flesh began to discolour.

After her solitary breakfast, Liz, armed with a local map, took a brisk walk. Many new houses had been built in the orchards of older ones, infilling here just as in the gardens of north Oxford. When she passed other people no one acknowledged her. She enjoyed greeting them with the two words she knew, '*Dzien dobry.*' The middle-aged and elderly were startled to be addressed by a stranger, and muttered something back; young Poles seemed far more friendly. Such, Liz admitted, were the judgements of a cursory traveller.

The Wolski Park was only ten minutes away. She was following one of the paths through the beechwood when she was stopped dead by a sound that turned her innards to liquid: the gut-deep roar of a lion. Liz scurried back to Andrew's home, an old woman running. He was awake, dressed in shorts and trainers.

'It must have escaped,' Liz gasped, the fear still trembling out of her. 'You have to tell them, quick.'

Her son laughed. 'Escaped from where?' he said. 'Kraków Zoo is in the middle of the wood. I'm off for my run. Think about what you'd like to do this afternoon.'

They took a boat trip on the Wisła. Other days they visited the Wieliczka salt mine, the Ojcowski Park. Andrew was not too proud to let his mother pay. He drove the hire car. They passed occasional cemeteries, every stone and marble grave festooned with flowers. 'This is how it is,' Liz said, 'when families live and die where they were born. Like your grandparents. In England we abandon the dead now, don't we?'

Andrew blanched, suggesting he thought she was getting at him, for his departure from the living.

'No, dear,' she said. 'I just mean it's impressive when the dead are honoured like this. Don't you think? They remain present.'

'Mum,' Andrew said. 'A hundred years ago four million Poles left this country.'

'Where did they go?'

'Well, America, mostly. All over. And they're leaving again.'

Unless he'd stopped seeing them while Liz was there Andrew seemed to have no friends. He took off for a solitary run, came back clutching his T-shirt, his slender torso – filling out a little now, in his late twenties – covered in sweat. He'd shower, before taking Liz out. His life was a lonely passage, it seemed, from one European city to another, in which he made no friends and left, she presumed, no trace. She did not enquire about romance. She never had; neither had Andrew ever volunteered information. A phrase, The Virgin Traveller, came into her head. Perhaps it was the title of some story she'd read.

In the Polish bathroom, the toilet was shaped to collect the occupant's evacuations in a dry bowl, there for all the world to inspect: when the lever was pulled to empty the cistern the contents were flushed down and off around the S bend. A disgusting design, Liz thought. She had to force herself to keep her gaze averted while operating the flush.

On Sunday morning, the day Liz was to fly home, she came in from the orchard with a bowl of pears, plums and blackberries, and found Andrew already dressed.

'You're up early,' she said.

'I'm going to church.' Andrew looked away from her as he spoke.

Now this was unexpected. Liz sat down at the kitchen table. 'I had no idea,' she said. 'Well, you know, I think … ' Her openness amused her. 'I think I'll join you.'

'You can't.'

'Excuse me?'

'I'm going to the monastery at Srebrna Góra. The church in the wood, with the towers.'

'Well, all right,' Liz said. 'I'll just come to the Mass if I may.'

Andrew reached to the cupboard for bowls. 'Women are only allowed in the church on certain feast days. Today isn't one of them.'

'Oh,' Liz said. 'I see. Well, fine. I'll just walk, as I was planning to.'

'Don't be like that, Mum,' Andrew said. 'Come on. You and Dad have always been against religion.'

'Your father more than me,' Liz said. 'And if you—'

'There is a painting in the church you'd like, though, in a side chapel. It's of Jesus being baptised.' Andrew laughed, a shy person's stifled chuckle. 'In the Vistula.'

Liz stoned the plums, cut up pears. They spooned yoghurt on the fruit and added pungent dark honey from the Tatra Mountains.

'The first time I visited the monastery,' Andrew said, 'I had no money with me. When I left, this monk stopped me and gave me an apple.'

Liz bit into a sour blackberry. She'd been here a week and with the daily walk and this holiday diet, felt healthier than she had in years.

'It's an order of hermits,' Andrew went on. 'Behind the church are stone cottages. The monks' cells.'

'What do they do all day?'

'They tend the vegetable gardens, gather fruit, make wooden tools.' Andrew took a mouthful of fruit and yoghurt, less chewed than tasted it, and swallowed. 'Mostly they stay in their cells. Reciting prayers, studying scripture. They used to wear hairshirts and whip themselves.'

'Why?'

'Why?' Andrew frowned. 'To mortify the flesh, of course.'

'Yes. No, but why?'

Andrew stopped, a spoonful of yoghurt midway to his mouth, and looked at somewhere around his mother's shoulder. If he wore spectacles, she thought, he'd be peering over them. A slight shake of the head, suggesting the difficulty of something somehow too simple, too obvious, to explain.

'They aspire to a life,' he said, 'of moral perfection.'

While Andrew celebrated his Catholic Mass, Liz took her final walk of the holiday, and came across a cemetery, the first seen not from a car but on foot. Bright red, yellow flowers on almost every grave. A generosity of commemoration; the departed not yet lost. She entered the graveyard, began reading the names and dates and looking at the photos embossed on many headstones, when suddenly she saw it. First the flowers on one grave, then on another. Although alone, Liz felt acute embarrassment, for the rubbish she'd spouted at her son in the hired car. Had Andrew known, and sat there at the wheel, saying nothing to contradict her? Surely he had. Liz looked around the cemetery, the flowers not so brightly coloured now, she realised. Many, in fact, if you peered closer, were old, faded, perishing. But all were made of plastic. A convenient way, she considered, to pretend to remember, but actually to forget.

That afternoon Liz flew home. She retrieved her Fiat from the medium-stay car park at Luton airport and drove back to Oxford. The sky was a muted blue, almost grey. She let herself into the house, called out John's name, waited for a reply. None came. In college, probably. Despite the fact that his diary was open by the phone, with the words *L back* scrawled upon today's page, it wasn't surprising that he'd not left a note. She was no longer hurt by such oversights.

At least there was food in the fridge, and bread not yet stale in the cupboard. Liz made herself a ham and cucumber sandwich, and ate it opening her post: gardening and clothing catalogues; bank, Visa, utilities information. She watered the geraniums, neglected this one dry week. Only then did she bump her luggage trolley up the stairs and wheel it into the bedroom. There she found John, dressed in his flannel pyjamas, spreadeagled upon the carpet as if he'd been clumsily dropped there. He'd been dead – according to the pathologist's subsequent report – for some thirty-six hours, felled by a massive coronary the previous morning.

***

The funeral, in the college chapel, was as secular as the chaplain could allow, but still ludicrously religious, Liz decided, for an atheist. But he would have wanted it in the academic if not ecclesiastical cloisters, his peers in gloomy attendance. Andrew remained in Poland: he'd just spent a week with his mother, he reasoned, his father would not miss him, and he had nothing to say to his sister. Sophie came up from Brighton and stood in goth black beside Liz, sobbing into a handkerchief, blowing her nose.

Obituaries appeared in three broadsheet newspapers, and in academic periodicals in the weeks thereafter, detailing a notable career. He was only sixty-two when he died but his important work was all done. Most of them closed with the words, *He is survived by his wife, Elizabeth, and their son and daughter*. Liz experienced a peculiar feeling with each one she read, almost as if she suffered some sort of hallucination, for the obituaries were inversions of John's life as it was known by those closest to him. If Liz were to write it, it would be about their courtship, wedding and honeymoon; their children; holidays, gardens, meals; particular evenings at the Oxford Playhouse or Sheldonian; certain friendships. At the end she might put, she thought, *He is survived by 'The Life of a Sixteenth-Century English Yeoman', and eight other books*.

***

She buried him in Wolvercote Cemetery, and once a week widened by a hundred yards the circuit of her constitutional to replace the flowers at his headstone. She and John had been companions who did not intrude upon each other's interior lives, but his unexpected death knocked her sideways. She lost her footing, did not really know who or where or why she was, for two, three months. She returned to work, she survived, but inside she was reeling. And then one day she realised that she'd stopped spinning, and landed not on the floor but on her own feet, somehow. 'There you are,' she said to herself, since there was no one else to say it to. 'You recover. There it is.'

That winter Liz planted a Victoria plum tree in the garden. She was unsure whether it was to commemorate her husband or a statement of intent to herself, a commitment to a diet of fresh fruit and yoghurt and honey.

The following June Andrew telephoned. 'I thought I'd come and visit,' he said.
'But that'd be marvellous.'
'In July.'
'Next month.'
'The week after next.'
'I can't wait.'

'I'll bring a friend,' he said. There was a pause, as Liz waited for him to say more. The silence lengthened.

'Give me the dates,' Liz said. 'Everything'll be ready.'

Andrew refused to be met, either at the airport or the coach station in Gloucester Green. A taxi brought him and his friend to the house. Liz rushed out to greet him. He'd cut his hair and shaved his beard, and looked – and felt in his mother's embrace – a little thinner than a year before. He stepped back. Liz turned to his companion.

'This is Monika, Mum. Monika: Elizabeth.'

The girl was blonde, slender, as tall as Liz, and strikingly pretty.

'Please, call me Liz. Everyone does.'

'Liz,' the girl said, as they shook hands. 'I am so happy to meet you.'

As they brought their luggage into the house Liz said to Andrew, 'I didn't know which room. Or rooms.'

'That's okay,' he said, heading straight upstairs as if he'd only left home last week. 'We'll sort it out.'

They came back down ten minutes later and laid out on the kitchen table presents for her. 'That honey you liked,' Andrew said.

'Bottle bilberries,' Monika said. 'This typical Polish fruit. And sausage is from my home region, in east of Poland, smoked, taken from young pig, Liz.'

'I had to bring you a packet of *pierogi*, Mum,' said Andrew. 'And a jar of *bigos*.'

'You shouldn't have, really,' Liz told them. She didn't say that the Co-op had started stocking Polish food on a stack of shelves; nor indeed that the pungent honey tasted different here. Too sharp, astringent. The jar she'd brought home a year before stood largely untouched in the cupboard.

Andrew took Monika off on sightseeing excursions, of historic Oxford entwined with his personal history.

'I like this Parks,' Monika told Liz. 'Where Andy climb in over railings.'

'Did you, Andrew? I don't remember that.'

'He show me tree he climb in night. When he is fifteen. Or fourteen.' Monika half-closed her eyes and began to swoon. Her face was perfectly proportioned. Her almond-shaped eyes and wide cheekbones gave her a kind of exaggerated, almost parodic, beauty. 'He like to sway in top, in moonlight,' she said. 'Is very nice, this Parks. Very nice.'

Monika slept in Sophie's room. Liz heard no movement along the corridor at night. The nature of their relationship was unclear. Andrew went off running, alone. Liz had taken the week off work, and Monika would find her in the sitting room, the kitchen.

'Please. I help,' she said. 'What are you doing?'

'I was just thinking about supper.'

Monika looked disappointed. 'Liz, I not like to do nothing. Please, give me job.'

Liz had been planning to redecorate the dining room. She'd already bought the paint, a cobalt-blue emulsion and some cream gloss, from the paint shop in Kidlington. Before she knew what was happening they had all the chairs up on the dining-room table, covered in dust sheets, and newspapers on the floor around the walls. Pictures were taken down, leaving the negative proof of their existence behind.

Monika was on a stepladder, cleaning the ceiling with sugar soap, while Liz sanded the picture rail, when they heard the front door. 'We're in here,' Liz called out.

Pages from the *Independent* ripped and curled up as Andrew opened the dining-room door. He stood there, his chest bare, clutching his sweaty T-shirt, appraising the situation. Then he smiled.

'The devil makes work,' Andrew said, gazing at the dust-covered mound in the middle of the room. 'Beat the devil.'

Monika applied herself with gusto. After the preparation, the next morning she found an old broom handle in the garage, rammed it into the handle of the roller, and painted the ceiling and walls. She attacked the physical work, Liz thought, like a man. Or like an Englishwoman, perhaps, of fifty years ago. As she worked, she talked, telling Liz how she and Andrew met.

'He is doing working for company I work for, stag parties in Kraków. You know stag parties, Liz?'

'Well, yes. I imagine they're much the same everywhere.'

'No, Liz. Please, Polish man not like this. This stag parties for English man, come to Kraków for weekend.'

'Ah, I see,' Liz murmured. She recalled an item on the radio: Brits abroad. Though wasn't that in Latvia, or Estonia?

'They come to drink, and do crazy thing like white water rafting, and then to drink some more.'

'You organise these trips?'

'I am escort,' Monika said. 'They have to have Polish girl with them, to take them from one pub to the other.' She laughed. 'I must pretend to like to drink, Liz.' She struck a pose, halfway between a shrug and a dance move, clutching the roller like a hoofer her cane. 'Party girl!'

'Did Andrew write the company's literature?' Liz asked. She was putting off applying the oil paint, with its chemical fumes; she'd always loved the chalky smell of emulsion.

'Andy do our website, very good English. He will show you on computer. Demand from English stags double. No. More. Double double, Liz. We are too popular. We have to hire more girls, and now Andy work for our company.'

'Andrew goes round the bars?'

Monika burst out laughing again. 'Liz. Please. Andy is monk. He is like those hermits he like to visit. I never

see him drink more than one beer. Never. But some
times, when stag party is too stupid, it's good to have
English man. To take them to consulate, or explain
them in the hospital.'

The women stood side by side, admiring the work
they'd done. Monika was sweating. Liz could smell the
meat she'd eaten today or yesterday, the *kabanos* or the
smoked ham. 'I know!' Liz said. 'Let's take a picnic to
the river.'

They drove out to Farmoor. The water was warm, and
all three of them swam. Andrew dived in from a willow
branch that hung out from the bank, but Monika only
dipped her toes in and made a girlish shriek of panto-
mime displeasure at the cold. Andrew floated over and
splashed her, and Monika drew her upper body into
a protective hunch. Liz couldn't quite interpret the
strange little performance: it seemed as if, after her
hard work, Monika felt she needed to realign herself
towards Andrew with feminine coquetry. But it was
odd, there was something overcompensating in it, and
Liz was glad when Andrew grabbed Monika and she
let him pull her into the water. Unclothed the girl was
not so slight as Liz had thought her, was loose-limbed,
athletic, a powerful swimmer. Liz watched her swim
off upriver.

Liz paddled about, came out and quickly changed, unhappily conscious of the ageing cellulite at the back of her thighs, the puckered flesh at her knees. She set food out on the rug. Bread and hams and cheeses, salad, fruit, wine. Andrew and Monika emerged from the river like a merman and his nymph, drops of water on their skin. Liz was struck by an idea she'd never allowed herself to entertain: that Andrew might not just survive, but even be happy. Was that possible? With this lovely, shallow young woman, with her energy and play and reproachful Slavic beauty. The thought, the idea of her son's happiness, made Liz shiver.

That evening Monika said, 'Andy. You show Liz website.'

'Oh no,' he said. 'No way.'

'I tell her,' Monika insisted. 'She want. You must.'

The three of them gathered around the large flatscreen monitor, Andrew and Monika pulling chairs, hemming Liz in. Monika brought forth images and information with her dextrous clicking of the mouse.

Kalashnikov shooting and five-a-side football weekend, Liz read.

'Also Zorbing,' said Monika. 'English man like this very much.'

Roll the stag down a hill strapped inside a large plastic ball. Laugh like crazy to drown out his screams of anguish and nausea. Sounds like fun? It sure is!

At the side of the screen appeared pretty young women, the evening escorts. 'There is Marta. This is Katarzyna. Look. Here is me.'

Yes, there was Monika. In a short black dress, surrounded by red-faced overweight men in tight T-shirts.

'Liz. Look. This one we just start one month ago.'

Mafia-style kidnapping. The best man arranges for the stag to be kidnapped. We provide three authentic hit men. We guarantee: the stag will be terrified.

'Very popular,' Monika said. 'Liz. Last week Jakub ill, guess what? Andy is Mafia hit man.'

Liz turned to her son, who grinned in an embarrassed way, and said nothing.

'This one,' Monika said. 'Not so popular.'

Auschwitz. A permanent reminder of the horrors of the Holocaust and what mankind is capable of. A full-on three-hour museum and site tour. It'll blow your mind. Recover back in Kraków with an evening drinking to forget. Round off the night dancing at the city's liveliest nightclub.

'There's always one or two get lost,' Andrew said. 'Between the clubs and the bars. Who stumble into the gutter and lie there. Jakub and I retrieve them from the police station in the morning.'

Liz shook her head. What had happened to her shy, thoughtful boy? He must have discerned her perplexity.

'Don't worry, Mum,' he said. 'Half the bars in Kraków have got signs up now: NO BRITISH STAGS OR HENS.'

'The hens are the worse,' said Monika. 'I refuse to work on them.'

'You've got to remember,' Andrew said. 'These English people. They're scum.'

After Andrew and Monika returned to Poland, the house was silent and empty in a way that it hadn't been before they came; nor after John had died. Liz remembered when Andrew was a teenager she'd pass his bedroom door and hear him singing the lyrics of tuneless songs. She'd pause there on the landing and listen, but could make out not a single syllable as her son copied in his tone-deaf way the obscure pronunciation of his favourite band's singer. As if this irked her memory, Liz would go downstairs singing to herself, the tuneful inanities of the pop songs of her own teenage years. 'Tell Laura I Love Her'. 'Poetry in Motion'.

One day, cleaning Andrew's room, Liz had found a booklet of lyrics. She switched the Hoover off and read them sitting at his cluttered desk. Calculator. Penknives. Binoculars. Airfix model planes still hanging from the ceiling. The lyrics were densely written, obscure but genuinely intriguing, with odd juxtapositions and thoughtful imagery. She'd felt strangely humbled, and rarely sang to herself again.

The following spring Liz was sixty years old. The GP practice held a retirement party in the house of one of the partners. More than fifty people came: doctors, nurses, health visitors, midwives, physiotherapists, her fellow receptionists. You didn't notice what a turnover of staff there was, how constantly people moved on, took maternity leave, retired; how many employees the practice depended upon, then did without. Her own replacement, Lucy, whose children were now at secondary school, was at the party. So, to Liz's surprise, was Sophie, contacted via someone's daughter someone knew. She didn't even look too out of place, wearing clothes cleaner and newer than Liz would have thought she owned, her hair no longer dreadlocked but short, and her skin defaced with fewer piercings than for ten or twelve years.

Liz was glad to have Sophie walk home with her, and stay the weekend. She brought her mother breakfast in bed, setting the tray on her lap, throwing open the curtains. Liz munched toast sleepily.

'The first day of the rest of your life, Mum. What are you going to do with it?'

Liz sipped the tea, coming slowly awake. She felt like she was being levered out of a depression she'd otherwise have slipped into; a depression she herself had not considered, but Sophie had.

'Do today, you mean?' Liz asked.

'No, I mean the rest of your life.'

Liz frowned. 'Well, I thought,' she began. 'I'd figured ... ' The home improvements, trips, evening classes she'd vaguely imagined seemed too pathetic to mention. She didn't want to admit: I was thinking of replacing the garden shed. I've always wanted to learn Italian. She swallowed the remains of the cup of tea. 'I have no idea,' she said.

'In that case,' Sophie said, 'we'd better concentrate on today. Let's go out somewhere. I'll treat you to lunch.'

Liz smiled in what she hoped was not a patronising way. 'You've got rich all of a sudden.' When she looked up, she saw Sophie nodding, wide-eyed, at her.

'I got offered a job,' she said. 'A six-month contract. Three of us, doing art projects with kids this summer. Art in the Parks.'

'Seriously?' Liz said. 'Here?'

Sophie grinned. 'Oxford.'

Andrew and Monika came back in July. Sophie was, unusually, at home when their taxi arrived. She gave her brother a long, tight hug, the kind that she surely remembered made him uneasy, an embrace inside which Andrew stood unresisting. Sophie and Monika kissed each other's cheeks, and carried bags inside.

The visitors unpacked their presents on the kitchen table. 'Liz,' Monika said. 'We bring some of your favourite.'

Liz watched aghast as Sophie ridiculed one item after another. 'You brought this stuff in your luggage? You are kidding, right? Sauerkraut? *Bigos*? Every supermarket in Oxford's got a Polish section, you numbskulls.'

It appeared to be the funniest thing Sophie had come across in months. The fact that she'd not seen Andrew in years, and only just met Monika, his friend, did not inhibit her for a moment. The others stared at the unprecious wares. Liz glanced at Monika's face: the lovely skin tightened over the jawline. Andrew looked embarrassed: he didn't lift his gaze from studying the grain in the wooden kitchen table.

'Mum could choose from six different kinds of sausage in Summertown alone.' Sophie shook her head as Andrew morosely unpacked a large jar of honey from layers of bubble wrap. 'You brought this by plane?' Sophie shrieked. 'There's a Polish restaurant on Cowley Road, we ate there after work on Wednesday.' She grimaced. 'Be honest,' she said. 'It's not exactly haute cuisine, is it? Dumplings for starters, dough in the main course and pastries for dessert.' She looked at Monika. 'How do you stay so slim?' Sophie asked. 'It must be one hell of a struggle, isn't it?'

Liz had gained a good impression, last year, of Monika's temperament. The tension in the room was such it felt like it would only be eased by something — plate, saucer — breaking. It seemed likely Monika might flounce off, at the very least; perhaps even hit out. Instead her clenched expression suddenly loosened. She smiled. Then she began laughing. 'Sophie. You are right. Yes, you are right. It is terrible. All the women of my mother's age, they look like the dumplings.' She turned to Liz. 'You are naughty,' she said, wagging her finger, still smiling. 'You should have told to us. Sophie, she tells us. Andy,' Monika said, 'I think we are a little bit stupid.'

Monika stayed, this time, in Andrew's room, though the pair displayed no other evidence of a more intimate relationship. Andrew spent time on his own, out walking, or reading at home, while Monika once again attached herself to Liz. They went together to the garden centre in Yarnton, where Monika helped choose a large summer house, and in the days before its delivery they emptied and took apart the old garden shed, which they transported in three trips in and on the roof of Liz's car to the waste recycling centre at Redbridge. 'You can't get anyone to do this kind of odd job any more,' Liz said. Heaving them with relish, Monika laid extra paving stones ready for the new summer house, which two men brought and put up the following afternoon.

Sophie came home from running her summer-holiday workshop in one of the municipal parks around the city, just as Andrew wandered in from a walk across Port Meadow.

'You all right?' one mumbled.

'Yeh. Okay?' the other responded.

'Why,' Andrew asked, 'do people always bang on about heaven?'

'Excuse me?' Sophie said. 'Like what people?'

'Every religion. Dream of heaven. Work for or wait for or wank for your reward in heaven.'

When she stopped and tried to look her brother in the eye, what first occurred to Sophie was to wonder what he'd taken. Acid. Mushrooms, maybe. That awestruck sensation.

'I've been out on the Meadow all day,' Andrew said. 'It's here, isn't it?'

'What?'

'Heaven. Heaven on earth.'

There was no sign of either Liz or Monika at home, though the car was in the driveway. Both Sophie and Andrew registered the distant laughter, but dismissed it as that of neighbours, until some distinctive high note coming through the kitchen window made Sophie say, 'That's your girlfriend, isn't it?'

They found them at the bottom of the garden, sat in green folding chairs in the otherwise empty, brand-new summer house, drinking champagne. The smell of wood, and wood preservative.

'Fetch two more glasses,' Liz said. 'And another bottle, from the fridge. Monika's helping me christen my new shed.'

Monika yelped with laughter. 'Liz. Is no shed,' she said. 'This your new summer residence.' Liz touched Monika's brown arm as if to beseech her to stop saying such funny things. 'This Liz place in the country,' Monika told Sophie and Andrew.

'Seriously, Mum,' Sophie said. 'Don't just fill it up

with rusty tools and old paint tins.'

'No,' said Monika. 'This Liz yoga room.'

'What are your plans?' Sophie asked, lighting a cig-arette. She sat by one of the summer house windows, and turned to blow smoke out of it.

Liz realised she'd not asked Andrew or Monika how their work was going, had not wanted to. *Is the stag business thriving?* No. She would have sounded just like John. Her son was gazing into the garden.

'Andrew?' Sophie said.

Andrew closed his eyes. 'What?'

'I said, What are your plans?'

Monika addressed Liz. 'I am sick of being escort for drinking men,' she said. 'Also, we have less work. Other companies more extreme. Like hunting stag, bridegroom, through forest with dogs.'

Andrew shook his head. 'We thought we might stay,' he said quietly.

'In England?' Sophie asked. 'Both of you?'

'You can stay here,' Liz said. 'Of course.'

Andrew turned to his mother. His gaze rested on the metal legs of her chair. 'If you're sure.'

Andrew drank water. The women grew jovial, their voices loud in the summer dusk. Liz reached across to her daughter, her middle- and fore-fingers outstretched from her fist, as if to propose a game of Scissors Paper Stone. 'Go on,' she said. 'Give me a puff.'

'Andy,' said Monika. 'I make lasagne. You heat up, please. Shall we have salad, too? Liz. Andy make very nice salad.'

Andrew walked across the lawn and disappeared into the dark house. A moment later lights came on. They could see him moving about in the kitchen, and watched in silence, as if witnessing a performance, a demonstration: *The Miracle of Electricity*, perhaps. *Homo sapiens Prepares a Meal*.

'You know,' said Monika, 'Andy doesn't work for months now.'

'His writing?' Liz asked.

Monika shook her head. 'I support him. No, I don't mind. Of course. But I think perhaps it will be better in England. For one thing, it will stop him going to see those monks.'

'Andrew's seeing monks?' Sophie wondered. She made them sound like illusions, like Andrew might be seeing things that weren't there.

'You mean those hermits on the hill?' Liz asked.

Monika nodded. She told them of the men with uncut beards and shaved heads, in their white habits, who never spoke; who'd repudiated bodily pleasures in order to achieve union with God, in silence and tranquillity. 'Andy goes to church and sits in pew. If monk goes in, to change cloth or flower, is enough for Andy. He gives him nod, you know, and he is content.'

Sophie copied Monika's imitation of this nod, exaggerating it further, into a rocking motion. 'Monks are social misfits,' she said. 'Sociophobes who don't know how to mix. Monasteries are social services; they've been providing residential care for centuries.' She stopped nodding. 'One wise abbot and a bunch of freaks. The same with convents. It's like Ashkenazi Jews have a high incidence of the genes for Asperger's, right? And the idea is the rabbinical tradition absorbs them. Picture them rocking backwards and forwards in their recitations from the Kabbalah.'

Sophie broke off to refill her glass. The emptied champagne bottle joined the others on the floor. Liz wondered whether her and John's secularism had in itself driven their children to rebel, towards transcendental solutions to the difficulty of being. In Sophie's case, to the chemical raptures, and oblivions, of drugs, sex, performance; in Andrew's, now, to religion. Would God ever disappear from the minds of men? Would the idea always be there, to catch men falling backwards?

Sophie was rocking her torso. 'Little Muslims in their madrassahs, too,' she said, 'rocking for Allah. Rock and roll, baby. You know AC/DC? See them on YouTube, Monika. Give the little Muslims air guitars, and let them rock away the blues.'

Monika was laughing, her cheeks swollen, her eyes filling with tears. The alcohol had smudged or distorted her and – because sober she was beautiful – rendered her eerie, almost grotesque. Or maybe, Liz admitted, it was the champagne's effect on her own perception. Which notion made bubbles of amusement rise from her own stomach.

'What are suicide bombers, for Christ's sake,' Sophie declared, 'but autistic victims of manipulative abusers? I mean, leave them alone. Religion gives a home to the miserable.' Sophie was away, riffing, finding new things coming out of her mouth, running after them, running after her tongue. Liz wondered whether she was still on any medication. 'How often do you hear of a suicide in a monastery? Never. They're full of at-risk individuals, right, who keep on going to a ripe old age. Self-harmers rendered harmless. It's a miracle.'

Monika nodded eagerly. 'I tell him,' she said.

'You tell him,' said Sophie.

'Yes, I tell him this.'

'I'll see how he's getting on,' Liz said. She cradled the empty bottles with her left arm, pincered glasses in the fingers of her right hand. She remembered a psychiatrist telling her many years before – half of Sophie's lifetime ago – that if they could help the girl through these difficult years then there was a good chance she could look forward to a slow calming of the storm. That her brain and body would draw towards a chemical equilibrium. 'The long view,' he said. 'Not much help now, but still ... '

Halfway across the lawn Liz paused. There was Andrew laying the kitchen table. She turned. It was that moment in the day when night has not yet fallen, the clear sky is indigo, there is light in the atmosphere but you cannot fathom where it comes from. Sophie and Monika were strange shapes lurking inside the wooden building. The orange glow of Sophie's cigarette when she inhaled. Liz's new summer house seemed to be floating at the edge of the lawn, as if it had been brought to her by river, towed down the Thames; it would remain tethered here for an endless succession of summer evenings. Neither she nor her children would be lonely. They would drink champagne and reap the harvest of their days.

The only sound was the intermittent drone of traffic on North Way, and the ring road further afield, but Liz heard a click and a scrape behind her. She turned back to the house as Andrew leaned out of the kitchen window and called, 'Ready.'

'Coming,' she replied. If she hadn't been standing here, Liz reckoned, they'd never have heard him. But she was, so she in turn called over her shoulder, 'Sophie. Monika. Supper's ready.'

To Liz's great surprise Monika, rather than Andrew, rose early the following Sunday morning and cycled on John's old bike to church, first to St Gregory and St Augustine just down Woodstock Road, then on to the Polish Mass at Blackfriars in St Giles. A week later she attended the Oratory at St Aloysius and Our Lady's Parish Church on Hollow Way. At each church she lingered afterwards and introduced herself to those she overheard speaking in Polish. During the week in between, Monika followed up and extended contacts she made, feeding information into a mobile phone and further details into a Lever Arch File with multicoloured tab dividers. She went to the Polish restaurant Sophie had mentioned, and the connected deli next door, but came back disappointed.

'Sophie,' she said. 'Why do you say this place is Polish? This woman is Russian. And her *husband*,' she said, with disdainful emphasis, 'he is from Ukraine.'

On the Wednesday Sophie hired a van and Monika accompanied her to Hastings, and Eastbourne, and other places along the south coast, where Sophie retrieved possessions scattered among the more or less permanent homes of friends and acquaintances. Reeling in the boundaries of herself. They returned to Oxford late in the evening, but within ten minutes Monika had freshened up and was back out, cycling to a club in town, for a Polish night she'd seen advertised on posters attached to lamp posts.

Liz was as intrigued as she was impressed by Monika's energy. She surely had a plan. Liz waited. It didn't seem likely that Andrew was a part of it. He remained behind in the room Monika left early each morning; walking to and from the summer house with a table, plants, a cabinet she stocked with crisps, nuts, olives, Liz caught sight of Andrew sitting at the window, gazing out across the back gardens, past the old fruit trees and the sun-tired lawns.

If not involved, at least Andrew remained active, leaving the house once a day for long walks from which he'd return with his eyes wide and unfocused. Tired, perhaps, Liz hoped, until, cycling down to Summertown, she saw her son standing on the pavement on the other side of Banbury Road, watching the traffic go by. Or rather, it appeared to her, from the way he seemed both observant yet preoccupied, watching the space between the traffic going by.

'Why don't you just call it Warsaw Workers or something?' Sophie asked. 'Kraków Cleaning Company?'

'No, no, no,' said Monika. 'Must be polite name, with Oxford in.'

'But everyone knows what good workers Poles are. Everyone wants a Pole working in their house. They may not want them in the country, but they want them in their own home.'

Monika shook her head. 'Sophie. You don't understand. We want to make friends, not enemies.'

Monika had made a poppy-seed cake for tea. Liz thought it was chocolate, until the first chewy and disappointing mouthful. The three women sat around the kitchen table.

'Liz. Only think about it,' said Monika. 'I ask you.'

'It's a brilliant idea,' said Sophie. 'You'd make a perfect team.'

'For sure.'

'I'm touched,' Liz said. 'I mean, I'm interested. Retirement does seem awfully premature, now that I'm stuck in it.'

It was only afterwards, after Monika had had cards and flyers printed for OXFORD ODDJOBS, with each of their names embossed – *Director Monika Nowacki*. *Administrator Elizabeth Mitchell* – and had delivered the first five hundred by hand, through letter boxes of houses in streets fanning out from their own, that it occurred to Liz that it could have been her daughter's suggestion that Monika involve Liz in the enterprise. But if so, she reasoned, why not? Monika wouldn't agree unless she wanted to, that was clear; she was too steely to be coerced to such an end.

In the early days of the business that summer, Elizabeth Mitchell began to imagine that she was herself a budding entrepreneur. She and Monika cleared out John's study. Andrew had made a brief inspection of his father's desk. 'I don't want anything,' he told the wall, and declined to help them. Instead he rummaged amongst the store above the garage, and retrieved archaic camping equipment: a canvas tent, a camp bed, which he fiddled around with on the lawn.

Liz gave the books to John's college library, though she wondered how much of a gift it was: history books seemed to pass quickly from favour, superseded by archaeological and other discoveries, by new ways of looking at the past.

'Of course they're useful, Mum,' Sophie assured her. 'They'll inform future historians about the authors' own times.'

The two young women helped Liz clear out other of her late husband's possessions. Monika emptied the chest of drawers and wardrobe into piles on the floor of the bedroom. Sophie divided the clothes into binbags for either charity shop or refuse, pausing to share memories evoked by a pair of cords, some pink woollen socks. Liz held on to a hat John wore on walks. A particular wide-checked shirt, his smell no longer present in the fabric, she admitted, two years on.

In the study, now the office of Oxford Oddjobs, Liz presided, taking calls from residents in the roads around her, arranging visits from Monika, hiring Polish labourers. Their system was simple: they charged £12 per hour, whatever the work – gardening, cleaning, building – of which they paid the worker £7. Of the £5 they kept, Liz received £1, Monika £2, and £2 went back into the business. In the beginning they shared office and printing costs, but they earned it back within weeks as people responded to their flyers, or called to say that so and so had recommended them.

The demand failed to surprise or daunt Monika. She conjured workers from an underworld of Polish migrants. Zsigmund, a highly qualified engineer from Poznań, did gardening. Women of all ages – Ella, Marta, Matylda, Dorota – cleaned the houses of liberal Englishwomen who'd not realised they could afford, or should employ, a cleaner. Kazimierz was a plumber, Stanislaw a carpenter, Radek an electrician, though if needs be any of them could do everything else, it seemed.

***

Monika was a calm dynamo, meeting clients, hiring employees, occasionally, when someone failed to turn up somewhere, cycling over, rolling her sleeves up and getting stuck in. One afternoon she and Liz both rushed round to a garden in Upland Park Road, to tidy the clippings of a long laurel hedge their gardener had abandoned. Seeing the way Monika stuffed the leaves into plastic bags, squeezing ever more in, brought back to Liz the image of her mother, working in their village garden with an energy that was emphatic, without doubt. The two women worked into the evenings. Sophie cooked supper if she was around. She had a new job, as a Youth Outreach Worker, and rushed in and out at odd hours. Andrew kept out of everyone's way. 'It's too complicated here,' he said. 'It's not simple enough,' he muttered, retiring to the tent on the lawn.

After lunch one day Liz laid some yellow roses on John's grave, and took her now only occasional walk around the lake. On the pavement outside two houses were boxes of apples, with signs saying HELP YOURSELF. Few had. The traffic on the big roads grew ever heavier, and so more adept in its effect upon Liz. She felt soothed, useful, included. It was strange, she thought: in all her years at the GP practice, money never crossed the reception desk. Money was numbers on the computer and on printouts; figures in columns that added up or failed to, in budgets that balanced or over- or under-spent, inseparable from those around it. No single sum – even her own wages, which went directly into her bank account – meant anything in itself.

Now cash shivered through her fingers, and the reality of it was thrilling. She made primitive piles of notes and coins. The workers came to the house and she handed them envelopes, which they opened neatly and whose contents they counted slowly. This money meant something to these people. They slept on the floor, three or four to a room, in the estates around Oxford, and sent all they could afford back to the home they couldn't wait to return to, or else saved it for a new life here.

Her own salary, too, Liz paid herself in cash and kept in her purse, so that she ceased having to draw on her pension or her savings.

In October, as the leaves fell from the trees, and the length of days contracted, and the nights grew chilly, Andrew disappeared. No one really noticed at first, so spectral had his presence been around the industrious ambit of the three women's lives.

'Where's Andrew?' one would ask.

'Oh, he must be in the tent,' another would answer.

'It's not there.'

'Maybe out on the Meadow.'

When he'd not been home for two days and nights, Sophie went looking for him. It was a Saturday. She cycled up Woodstock Road and into Upper Wolvercote, down around the Green and over the railway line. She chained her bike to the iron railings and set off across Port Meadow. The smell of smoke: a pale wisp rose from an old bonfire on the allotments. Seagulls wheeled greedily. Were they pausing in the centre of England on their way east or west, from the Irish to the North Sea? Sophie wondered. Or had they become accustomed to a life inland? In the misty distance horses were lazily grazing. One or two joggers, people walking their dogs. No one looked as though they were here of their own free will, somehow, except for a man talking on a mobile phone as he strolled. Plotting, she thought, with his illicit lover, in the wide freedom of the Meadow.

Sophie climbed the bank and entered Burgess Field, the old dumping ground that had been covered in topsoil and turned into a nature reserve. It was a bare heath but for spinneys and thickets of trees planted here and there, which had grown to twice the height of a woman. After half an hour wandering Sophie saw the khaki tent, in a clump of birch and pine trees. Inside, a sleeping bag, a thick blue blanket, and a Bible. The smell of damp canvas. There was no sign of Andrew but there was no doubt it was his. Attached by white cotton to the top front of the tent was a piece of cardboard on which in black felt-tip were written the words *Domine meus me non damnant.*

The women ate carbonara. Liz had bought a Rioja reserve from 1998, with the cash in her purse. The cork was purple-black, impregnated with the wine, and withdrew gracefully from the bottle. Sophie recounted to the others her expedition.

'It means God, or Lord, or My God,' said Liz. 'My Lord, do not *damnant*.' She pressed her left index finger to her temple, as if to stimulate her memory there. Or perhaps to shoot it for failing her. 'Condemn me.'

'He didn't have anything,' Sophie said. 'Nothing to cook on. To clean with.'

'Andrew,' said Monika, with an air of possessive authority. 'I know him. He will come back when is cold.' She looked from Liz to Sophie, their doubtful faces. '*Really* cold.'

That week Liz attended two day-courses run by Oxfordshire Business Enterprise, for people starting up their own small business. On the first, she was given an overview of keeping financial records; preparing a business plan, doing market research and creating a marketing strategy; costing and pricing the company's services; cash-flow forecasting and profitability; taxation, National Insurance and VAT.

Liz had always assumed that budding entrepreneurs simply started trading, as she and Monika had done. Seeing what it really took to run a business, she felt the shape of the challenge ahead. 'We should have thought a lot more before we began,' she told Monika.

'This what we done,' said Monika. 'It was market research already.'

'Well, better late than never.'

The first course took place at Exeter Hall in Kidlington. The second, two days later, was at the Colin Sanders Innovation Centre in Banbury. There Liz learned in more detail how to administer the finances of a company. Allowable business expenses; efficient paperwork; accounting systems. Keeping track of costs, cashflow, profit.

Liz drove back to Oxford, her head reeling. She was too old to learn so much. Far too old. But she'd do her best. She was a trier, she had to admit. She'd not give up on it herself. She was halfway home when she realised she'd failed to take advantage of being so close to the village she'd grown up in. Her parents were buried there, and it would have been good to visit their grave. She felt like she'd vaguely betrayed them; had betrayed herself, too.

On Sunday morning, after the clocks had gone back, Liz set off from the house on foot. She walked to Port Meadow and across to Burgess Field, then followed Sophie's directions. There was a mild drizzle, of the kind you were less aware of falling than of finding, tiny droplets, on your clothes, and on your skin. With the leaves turning, and dropping from the trees, it took Liz a while to see the khaki tent even after she'd found its location. She made the steps towards it with trepidation, uncertain what she would find. There was something wild about it here, like a fairy tale, as if it might turn out to be the home not of her son but of some man of the woods he'd been transformed into.

She called out, 'Andrew?' as she approached. There was no answer. She stood outside the tent, and spoke his name again. 'Andrew?'

No reply came, but she heard a sound from inside, a shuffling of blankets or clothes. Emboldened, Liz lifted the tent flap. There was Andrew, in his sleeping bag. He covered his head with his hands like a teenager, as if she'd thrown open the curtains on a sunny morning, and made a grunting objection. She saw a black Bible, and recognised a red torch she kept in her bedside table.

'I've brought you croissants, Andrew. And I've a Thermos of coffee. Will you join me for Sunday breakfast?'

Liz leaned in out of the wet. The smell was teenage, too: unwashed maleness, and old canvas. She figured she'd rather put up with the soft rain than the hostile odour. 'I'll wait out here,' she said.

They sat outside, Liz on the blue blanket. Andrew had unzipped his sleeping bag and wrapped it around himself like a thick cloak. He ate three croissants, stuffing one after the other into his mouth, chewing arduously. The coffee he forgot until it was cold, then he downed it in one.

'Will you come back home?' Liz asked. 'We worry about you outside.'

Andrew wiped his hand across his mouth. He was unshaven, and dark-eyed, and gazed at the damp ground as he spoke. 'It's good here.'

'I'd so like to see you warm,' she said.

Andrew laughed, a kind of bitter, dismissive laugh that seemed to suggest that warmth was the most trivial, even decadent, of human needs. 'It's better without people.'

'What's better, Andrew?' she asked.

'To live alone with God,' he said. 'And for God alone.'

When she saw that he was not prepared to come home with her, Liz said, 'I've got more food here I'll leave with you.'

'I have given you every plant yielding seed which is upon the face of all the earth,' Andrew said. 'And every tree with seed in its fruit; you shall have them for food.' He raised his head and indicated with staccato nods various directions. 'Apple trees,' he said. 'Hazelnuts. And mushrooms.' He laughed to himself again. 'I know where they are.'

Liz took the bag from her rucksack, and when she placed it by the tent Andrew did not object. She was sure he did not wish her to embrace him; she only took one of his hands in hers, and squeezed it, before she left.

November was miserable, but the last weekend of the month the clouds lifted and the sun came out to shine weakly on the grey city. On Saturday Sophie took food

and spare clothes to Andrew; she and her mother alter-
nating biweekly visits. Monika indulged them. 'He will
come,' she insisted. 'When is really, really cold.'

Liz remembered the roofs of the houses in Kraków:
metal plates stood up from various points across them.
Andrew had explained to her that every winter snow
built up thickly on the roofs. The plates were there to
break the snow up as it melted. Otherwise a huge slab
might slide off the roof and bury someone stood below.
Monika, Liz feared, might have a more demanding
definition of cold than most.

On Sunday morning, as the three women ate breakfast together, plain croissants and *pains au chocolat*
from Taylors, Monika put down her teacup and said,
'Enough.' The others waited for her to expand. 'I work
every day for twelve weeks now. No. Thirteen. Today I
take holiday. You know, Liz, what I like to do?'

Liz shook her head, and shrugged expectantly.

'Your village,' Monika said. 'Your parents. I like to
see. Shall we go? Maybe Sophie come also.'

Sophie frowned regret. 'I said I'd see Joe today,' she
said. 'The playwright? He's writing this play, I said I'd
read through it with him. Shame. I've not been there
in years.'

Liz cruised up the A4260 rather than join the M40. She
bought flowers from a filling station, a bouquet of white
and pink carnations. Monika switched on the radio,
searched for channels, settled for one featuring pop

music. The presenter got very excited about each ditty he played. The lyrics were all as inane as those of the songs of Liz's distant memory. *Never gonna leave you, baby, this one's gonna last forever.* She wondered whether there'd been a brief period of complexity, ingenuity, in the story of popular song, that coincided with her son's youth.

'I wonder if it's time,' Liz ventured, 'for us to do something.'

'About Andy,' Monika said without hesitation. 'You mean doctor.'

'He may need to be brought in,' Liz said. 'For his own safety.'

She could just register Monika nod beside her. They drove on without speaking. A car overtook her, beeping its horn and cutting in aggressively. Presumably she'd annoyed the other driver by how slow she'd been drifting north.

The village was little changed. Houses built of dark brown stone, a small estate of brick bungalows. Liz showed Monika the cottage she'd been brought up in. 'There was a shop there,' she said, pointing across the stream that ran beside the road. 'And that used to be a post office.'

There was hardly anyone around. On a Sunday morning fifty years ago most everyone would have been in church, and any moment now would come stuttering into the autumn morning, spreading out through the village, bringing it back to life. Today, though, the church was empty, its front door locked. The inhabitants of the village remained inside their quiet houses or had left already, in pursuit of leisure opportunities in the world around. Shopping, football, fishing, golf, car boot sales ...

After some minutes' uncertain searching, Liz found the headstone, towards the corner of the graveyard, close to the thorn hedge. Her memory had shifted it, nearer to the church. For some further minutes, until her brain had recalibrated the scene, its location felt uncannily wrong.

Victor Mitchell, 1915–1989
and Phyllis Mitchell, 1919–1992
One is closer to God in the garden
Than anywhere else on earth

Liz laid the flowers on the grey stone. She'd had the sentiment inscribed in deference to her mother. When John had made fun of it, she'd cringed, feeling much as he did. Now, it seemed less superstitious than a statement of modest fact. There were no other mourners in the graveyard. A number of standing crosses, she noticed, had been brought down upon their graves, as if by a great storm. She felt Monika beside her take hold of her arm.

'Liz,' she said. 'Have I told you? My parents, I do not know, they are alive or they are dead?'

Reaching her free hand across her body, Liz took Monika's arm.

'It is long story,' Monika said. 'My father. When I leave, to go to Kraków, he say, "You go now, never come back." My mother is crying, my sister. What life is for me there? My brother walk with me but father pull him back. He shout after me again, "Never." I don't turn round.'

'I'm so sorry.'

She felt Monika shrug beside her. 'It is this, what it is.'

The two women, their arms entwined, stared at the headstone together, as if there was revealed here a deep familial connection between them.

'I've been thinking,' Liz said. 'Lately. And now I'm sure. When I die, I'd like to be buried here. Not with John, in Oxford, but here, with my parents. Is that awful?'

Monika didn't say anything.

'It feels as I get older that I'm drawing closer to them all the time,' Liz said. 'It's terribly strange.'

Monika squeezed Liz's arm. 'I will remember,' she said. 'Only please: not yet. Okay? First, you must help me make business.'

Liz laughed weakly. 'I shall do my best.'

'We make super business,' Monika said, turning from the grave. 'Businesswomen of Year. I can see awards on shelf in summer house.'

'South of England, Best New Company. You can make a speech, Monika.'

They walked between headstones, from the grass to the gravelled path.

'Liz. Maybe we employ another person in office soon. What do you think?'

'To concentrate on the accounts?'

'Yes. And maybe is time for advertising. In newspaper. But which one?'

At that moment the bell in the church tower rang, activated by a timed mechanism, the first of twelve doleful chimes. Liz registered them briefly, a sound that was more like a memory than a present reality, before returning her attention to Monika beside her. The pair strolled out of the graveyard, towards the car, scheming and teasing the future, turning from mortality back to this world, and hope of the life to come.

Hunters in the Forest

Ben cocked the rifle and placed the barrel, wrapped in a towel, in the vice. Cobwebbed windows, murky garage light, the petrol-sweet stink of the lawnmower. He folded a length of fishing line, threaded it into the breech.

He cut a white T-shirt into inch-square patches, wet one with solvent and dragged it along the barrel with the fishing line pull-through. The white cotton smudged with grey. He repeated the operation with fresh patches and solvent, then pulled dry patches through, till one came out of the muzzle clean as it had entered.

Ben had owned this gun eight years now. A present from his father on his tenth birthday, he'd unwrapped it and known wonder. Had staggered outside: used up all hundred pellets in the box, shredded targets, in an orgy that left the barrel so hot his spit on it sizzled.

The rifle was too big for the boy, but he grew into it. He'd camp with his father along the Teign river, shoot rabbit or pigeon, roast their prey over an open fire. Ben became a crack shot, winning annual prizes for his shooting at Christow Agricultural Show, kudos that saved the studious boy from teasing.

The gun grew up with him. The weekend after Ben's last O level exam his father took him to a gunsmith in Exeter who'd replaced the beech stock with oiled walnut, put in a new trigger mechanism and mounted a telescopic sight. Hard to believe it was still only an air rifle suitable for target practice and despatching small vermin; it looked like a mighty weapon.

On a final piece of cloth, Ben fed a dribble of fine grease through the barrel, a lubricant that would add a degree of chiselling to the pellets' passage. As a rust prevention he wiped the metal surfaces of the gun with WD-40. Finally he worked a little oil into the wood, inhaling the scent of linseed.

With an armful of empty cans, Ben paced to the end of the garden, rifle over his shoulder, lead pellets loose in his pocket. After cleaning, it would take ten or twenty shots to settle the rifle down. He cocked it, loaded a pellet, snapped the barrel shut, took aim, fired. The recoil, infinitesimal, nudged his shoulder. In the gathering dusk the pellets dented the cans with dull *thock*s.

Ben tiptoed through the house in the dark, pulled his boots on at the back door, hauled bags out to the lane. Stars still hung in the black sky. In the quietness he heard a front door slam at the top of the village even before he heard Phil kick-start his bike, then gun the engine: it spluttered, with the choke out, then fired into glorious full-throated life.

Ben tracked the bike's progress as it growled its way down from the council houses. It swung around the corner by the post office and the beam found him. He raised his hand to shield his eyes.

Phil switched off the engine. Sat astride the bike, feet on the ground, the teeth of his grin visible. 'What the ell you got there?' he said.

'Food. Sleeping bag,' Ben said. 'Tent.' The gun was in a sheath, slung over his shoulder. Phil's rifle, he could see, was in a scabbard attached to the side of the bike.

'This here's a chopper, bud, not a caravan. We're only stoppin out one night. Leave the tent behind.' He leaned into a pannier, drew out a scratched old helmet. 'Better wear this.'

They pulled away, choke out again: the fumy rich mixture. Ben rode pillion with his hands behind him, gripping the metal bracket at the back of the seat, as he'd seen other male passengers do.

At Gidley's Turn they joined the valley road, and Phil opened up the throttle. Ben felt suddenly, horribly, precarious.

'I need to hang on,' he yelled, and though he did not know whether Phil could hear him, he put first one, and then the other, arm round Phil's waist. Like one of the other man's girls. He was still chuffed at being invited on this trip: telling Phil in the Artichoke that he was off soon, Phil said Jimmy was too, the three of them should mark the leaving. Ben could smell the patchouli in the leather of Phil's jacket. He realised he was committing a grave offence, that this was a ruinous way to begin the excursion. But there was a cool draught of air coming off the river this late September morning, the Kawasaki chased its headlight barrelling through the darkness, and he wanted to live to see his nineteenth birthday.

Jimmy's family lived out beyond Doddiscombsleigh, up a dried mud and pebble track, bumpy and potholed. Phil slowed to a crawl. Rusted ghosts of vehicles either side of the track. After a slow half-mile the beam lit up what looked like an assortment of shacks and sheds tacked together. Mismatched windows, odd doors.

Phil switched off the headlight and killed the engine. To Ben's surprise, it was no longer dark. The stars had dissolved into a cloudless sky. A door opened. In grimy blue jeans, bare-chested, with shoulder-length hair, Jimmy appeared, squinting out at them, scratching a nipple with one hand. Rough tattoos on the knuckles, a skull on his muscular torso.

'You two's bright an early,' he said, croaking. He yawned. 'Come an have a bite a breakfast.'

'Don't want to disturb no one,' said Phil.

Jimmy rubbed his eyes, and turned back inside. 'Old man's out,' he said over his shoulder. 'Stick the kettle on.'

The door by which they entered gave directly on to a large room. It had a stove, stainless-steel sink; draining board, shelves, table all of unplaned wood. The floor was strewn with children's toys, scrappy items of clothing. A sweet odour.

Along one wall a sagging red sofa. On the windowsill behind it a dozen empty Coca-Cola bottles, from one of which a wasp was trying to escape. It kept reaching up as far as the elegant neck and then fluttering back to the bottom, where it sucked a little more sugar from the sticky remnant there before trying again.

'Hot enough for you lads?' Jimmy's mother asked. Short, broad, with green eyes and winter-pale skin, as if she'd spent the whole of this long summer indoors. She spread butter on to the white loaf before cutting each slice. The tea was strong and sweet. On Ben's tongue the enticement of bacon frying. Jimmy's mother stepped across from the stove with the frying pan and scooped two rashers each on to their bread. Butter melted beneath hot oily meat.

Phil munched, and mumbled, 'Bacon sarnies,' nodding with appreciation and gratitude. Ben murmured in agreement. As the boys ate, a succession of people wandered drowsily into the room. They ranged in age from infancy to youth and shared Jimmy and his mother's pale muscularity; they came and sat at the table, waiting to be fed, gazing at Ben with their gooseberry eyes. Phil winked and grinned at them.

A dog lolloped in from outside, a thoroughbred springer spaniel. It sat beside the stove staring up at Jimmy's mother, who ignored it until, all of a sudden, she tossed bacon rinds into the air which, jumping open-mouthed, the dog caught with a greedy snap of its jaws.

A man a little older than Jimmy appeared, even more squat and heavyset, with similar home-made tattoos. He poured himself a mug of tea at the other end of the table. 'Bit late to go huntin, innit?' he said. 'Or early. Be gone be time you're out.'

'Who asked your opinion?' Jimmy said, without looking up from his plate.

'Be gone back to bed theirselves,' his brother said, and chuckled at his own wisecrack.

Phil pushed his chair back. 'Best be off then,' he said, smiling. 'Reckon we'll keep goin all day on that,' he told Jimmy's mother.

As Ben stood up, a young woman came into the kitchen. She carried a wan, blond infant on her hip, but she herself had jet-black hair, deep brown skin, dark eyes. It struck Ben that she had been abducted, in order to revitalise this family's gene pool. There was pathos in her failure. He reckoned she might be younger than he himself was; certainly, she was the prettiest girl he'd ever seen. He tried not to stare at her, but his lowered eyes kept raising themselves, avid for beauty. Phil tickled the baby, said it was better than anyone else here, teased its mother and Jimmy's brother both, undaunted. The girl smiled shyly, the brother drank his tea.

Jimmy rode his Triumph around the side of the house. He paused, put two fingers between his teeth, and whistled. The spaniel came dashing out of a side door, bounded into the air and landed in the home-made pannier attached to Jimmy's bike. Ben laughed out loud. Jimmy scowled.

'You ain't goin a bring that yappin springer a yours?' Phil demanded.

'Not leavin her here, am I?' Jimmy told him.

'She'll fright off any deer fore we ever find em.'

'Don't matter, then, do it, cos there baint no deer in them woods.'

'I told you, Joe Cornish saw em t'other mornin.'

Jimmy gave his throttle a twist. 'I never seen em,' he yelled, and he eased his bike forward and out along the track, weaving his way between potholes, Phil tracing the route close behind.

They rode along the valley then headed up towards Moretonhampstead, climbing steadily. The little town was wide awake: shops open, a brewery lorry delivering beer to one of the pubs. Ben heard a metal keg clang as it hit the pavement.

They carried on beyond, up towards the moor. Along narrow, high-hedged lanes, wooden stands for milk churns outside farms: Thorn, Higher Stiniel, Yardworthy. The dog sat high in the pannier, eyes closed against the wind, long ears blown behind her.

They followed a dead-end road around the edge of the reservoir to an empty car park, manoeuvred the bikes through a little gate and sidled into the forest along a wide track. After half a mile they eased off to the right on a path between overgrown shrubs that brushed against them. When the path opened into a small clearing, Ben got off, the dog jumped out of the pannier, Jimmy and Phil walked their bikes under the trees.

'Good a spot as any,' Jimmy declared. His dog dashed wildly about, sniffing the ground.

'Can't argue,' Phil said, taking three cigarettes from his pack. He flicked open the top of his Zippo lighter, set his thumb to roll the cog that struck a spark off the flint. The other two leaned towards him. 'Watch the dog-ends,' Phil said. 'Don't want to start a forest fuckin fire.'

'Slip in, slip out,' said Jimmy, exhaling his first drag. 'Leave no trace.'

The spaniel ran further along the path, where dry grass grew waist high, and sprang, ears flapping.

Phil drew his rifle from its scabbard. He took bullets from a box and eased them into pouches along his leather belt. Ben stuffed his denim jacket in the pannier.

'Another hot day for sure, this,' Phil said, draping his leather jacket across the bike saddle. He had on a black T-shirt. His face and wiry arms were deeply tanned, his long brown hair had been bleached and corkscrewed by the sun. He was still skinny, despite two years already spent labouring for a pig farmer near Hennock.

Ben took his own gun out of its sheath. Phil stared as Ben checked the scope was in place.

'Is that what I think it is?' Phil asked. 'Let's have a look.'

Phil put his cigarette in his mouth and scrutinised the rifle, eyes screwed up from the smoke. He held it out for Jimmy to see. 'Know what this beauty is?' he asked. Jimmy said nothing. Phil brought the gun down over his knee, cocking it, pulled the spring tight. 'Rolls-Royce with a Mini fuckin engine.' He closed the rifle, pointed it at the sky and squeezed the trigger, blasting air upwards. 'What the fuck's you goin a bag with this?' he asked Ben. He was grinning the whole time, like Ben had come thus armed purely, and thoughtfully, for Phil's amusement.

'Leave him be,' Jimmy muttered.

'While you two are blundering around after non-existent deer,' Ben said, 'I thought I'd catch a couple of rabbits so we've got something to eat tonight.'

'What you reckon, bud?' Phil asked Jimmy. 'Reckon he could pick off a bunny or two with this here toy?'

Jimmy was easing something out of his own gun case. It wasn't a rifle, of any kind, but a long, narrow strip of wood. Jimmy grasped it around the middle, where string was wound tightly.

Phil shook his head, still grinning. 'You is pullin my plonker, bud. What happened to the old man's gun?'

Jimmy secured a loop of string around one end of the length of wood. 'Bastard hid it.' He flipped the bow around and put the end against his foot, bent the top towards him. 'Fucked if I care,' he said as he took the strain of the bow, wincing, and tried to string it. 'What you think Englishmen used for huntin,' he grimaced, 'before guns was invented?' The tension in the bow, the pressure Jimmy was forced to exert to bend it, made the end of it tremble in his hand, so that he couldn't pop the loop of string over. Sweat broke out on his forehead. 'Used bow and arrow for hundreds a fuckin years,' he gasped.

Ben stepped across and took the string from Jimmy, freeing him to use both hands to hold the bending bow. It stopped trembling, and Ben secured the string.

'We goin a stand around all day yackin?' Phil said. 'Let's crack on.'

They crept through the trees in loose formation, the spaniel running ahead, too excited by the scents her nose detected to obey Jimmy's commands. He removed his belt and looped it through her collar. The dog strained forward incessantly, choking herself, rasping. Jimmy kept yanking her back. 'Not used a bein on a lead.'

After an hour they paused. Ben took out his Marlboros, opened the packet and offered it towards the others. 'What are you planning to do with her,' he asked, 'when you join your regiment?'

'Takin her with him,' Phil said. 'Run point with Jimmy's gang a squaddies, on the streets a Belfast.'

'Fuck you,' Jimmy said.

'Sniffer dog, get her into bomb disposal, I should,' Phil continued. 'Got one hell of a nose.'

'Leave her alone,' Jimmy said. The spaniel loped over to him. 'Don't you take no notice a they,' he said, scratching her tummy. 'They knows nothin about dogs. You go on, girl, flush them deer out for us.'

The forest was a thousand acres of conifers planted fifty years earlier on moorland. Ben identified old Japanese larch, Norway spruce, lodgepole pine. They stepped out of cool plantations into the sun's bright glassy glare.

'Bloody hot, innit?' Jimmy said, sweating.

'Should a left your jacket with the bikes like we did,' Phil told him.

'Pah!' said Jimmy, as if to wonder what kind of fool Phil took him for. 'I int losin this leather,' he said, patting his jacket. 'Been through too much together.'

Ben knew they christened their black bikers' jackets with cider and piss, whisky, blood. Jimmy's had tassels down the arms. A white skull and crossbones were painted on the back. Clipped to the front were German World War Two medals and insignia, an Iron Cross and a swastika among them.

The plantations were criss-crossed by gravel roads and by streams of cold water running down off the high moor. Ben cupped his hands to drink; Jimmy lay and lapped, like his dog beside him. Butterflies wafted about them, as if studying these specimens of *Homo sapiens*. The sweet smell of pine sap.

'There are longhorn beetles,' Ben told his companions, 'that spend years as larvae. One can start its life in a pine tree in Russia and emerge as a beetle from the leg of a table in someone's living room in Exeter.'

'No shit,' said Phil.

Jimmy took a cigarette and threw his packet to Phil, who drew one for himself and threw the pack to Ben. The three of them gazed at the ground as they smoked.

'I'm tellin you,' Phil said. 'That's deer droppins.'

Jimmy shook his head. 'Tis a rabbit, you tosser.'

'Come on, bud,' Phil said, turning to Ben. 'You're the bunny killer. Ever see rabbit droppins this big?'

Ben knelt down. With a twig he turned a pellet over. 'A rabbit's is round. Look, this is oval, wouldn't you say? And look at these.' He nudged a different pellet. 'They've all got these tiny indentations at one end.'

Jimmy crouched, frowning. 'How the fuck do it make that, whatever it is?' he wondered. 'A little dimple in every droppin. That is weird.'

'I don't know,' Ben admitted. He stood upright. 'I tell you what. I'll get back to the bikes, set up camp, make a fire. Try and bag a rabbit or two. Reckon I'll have more chance on my own.' He realised it sounded like an accusation. 'I mean, it's what I'm used to.'

'Good idea, bay,' said Jimmy.

Phil was still kneeling on the path. 'I thought you hunted with your old man,' he mused.

'Next time I see Joe Cornish,' Jimmy said, 'remind me to ask if twasn't unicorns he saw.' He let his cigarette fall and stamped it out on the dry earth. 'Sod this for a bunch a soldiers.'

Phil stubbed his butt out on a stone. 'He was up here haulin a lorryload a wood for they sawmills over Kingsteignton. Don't worry, bud, we'll be takin enough venison back for your whole family.'

'Don't get lost,' Ben said, turning to head downhill.

By the time he'd skinned and butchered the rabbits the heat of the day had dissipated. Ben built a fire. Dry grass caught, twigs crackled aflame.

Ben looked in the motorbike panniers, but could find nothing except spare bullets and a bottle of whisky in Phil's, one of vodka in Jimmy's. In his own rucksack, wrapped in separate plastic bags, were tea, coffee, dried milk and sugar. With his Opinel penknife, bought while on a school exchange in Brittany the year before, he cut forked pieces of branch and stuck them in the ground either side of the fire; sharpened sticks and skewered the carcases; rested them in the wooden forks. The smell of burning meat made his stomach rumble. There could be no better compass, he thought, for Phil or Jimmy, or the dog.

He heard them shortly, crashing down through the plantation. Phil walked straight across the clearing past the fire to his bike, where he slid his rifle back in its sheath and found the whisky.

Jimmy patted Ben on the back. 'You're a fuckin star, bay,' he said. 'How many a they you got?'

'Four.'

'Smell it a mile away,' Jimmy said. 'Bay's a fuckin star.'

Phil came to the fireside with his leather jacket draped over his shoulders and sat on his haunches, gazing morosely at the flames. Jimmy went to his own bike. The dog sat staring at the meat. Phil unscrewed the bottle top, took a slug of liquor, and passed the bottle over to Ben.

'Don't know how people drink that stuff,' Jimmy said. 'Gives me the shakes, do whisky.' Addressing Ben, he said, 'Joe Cornish. Phil reckons he set us up.'

Phil stared at the fire. 'Told him us was goin a do somethin fore you two clears off. It was him suggested huntin, said he'd seen deer up here. Windin me up, wasn't he? Be down the pub tonight laughin at us.'

Jimmy took a cigarette, threw the packet across the fire to Ben. 'Phil got off with his bird last year, see. I told him Joe knew.'

Ben tossed the packet to Phil. Phil said nothing. He drew a twig from the fire, lit his cigarette with its glowing end.

'Lucky you ain't been give a kickin,' Jimmy said. 'Things you gets up to.'

A rueful smile began slowly to materialise on Phil's face. 'Tell you what, though, bud, she was nice, was Hayley. Worth bein sent on any wild goose chase for.'

'Worth it for you, maybe,' Jimmy muttered. 'Don't know what us got out of it.'

'Not much,' Ben agreed.

'Gives em that cheeky-little-boy smile of his, they falls over theirselves.'

Dusk gathered in the trees. Ben turned the skewers. Fat dripped off the meat, fell hissing in the flames. 'Wouldn't mind some trick like that myself,' he said.

'Don't you worry, bud,' Phil said. 'That's all they get up to at university, you lucky sod. Them brainy birds, be beggin for it. That there meat ready? Look at this.' He held his soggy cigarette up for the others to see. 'Salivatin so much my fag's ruined.' He dropped it in the fire.

'Nearly done,' Ben said. 'But unless you've got some hidden compartment on the bikes, we've got nothing else.'

'Like what?' Jimmy asked.

'I thought it was agreed that one of you would bring bread. The other one utensils.' Ben turned the meat again. 'I brought coffee and tea, but we need a pan. Mugs.'

'No one said nothin to me,' Jimmy claimed. He turned to Phil. 'Didn't tell me nothin, bay.' He took a swig of vodka.

'This is almost ready,' Ben said.

'Don't move,' said Phil, looking past the other two. Like a man miming stealth he tiptoed to his bike and pulled the rifle from its scabbard.

Jimmy and Ben turned gradually in the direction in which lay whatever Phil had seen. In the gloom, an obscure grey shape moved at the base of a tree.

'Pheasant?' Ben wondered.

'Partridge, innit?' Jimmy guessed.

'Where'd it go?' Phil asked. He yanked back the bolt of his rifle to load the bullet into the chamber, put his eye to the scope.

'Same place.'

'Got it.' Phil pulled the trigger. The bullet hit something that caused a fluttering of splinters, and there was the sound, a quick abrupt explosion. Phil fired again, and a third time.

'Must a hit it,' Phil said. The three of them trotted over. There was no sign of a carcase, nor of feathers or blood. They each looked up and around, peering into the black depths of the forest.

With Ben distracted by the phantom bird, the meat was charred, but Phil and Jimmy made no complaints. Ben had baked the rabbits' entrails on a stone placed in the centre of the fire. The spaniel swallowed these in a flurry of greedy mouthfuls, then sat beside Jimmy, watching him with sorrowful eyes. Occasionally he cut a morsel of flesh and fed it to her with his fingers.

Phil let out a long belch of appreciation, then set to rolling a roach: stuck three cigarette papers together, broke a No. 6 into it, then crumbled a little cannabis amongst the tobacco. He tore off an end of the Rizla cardboard and screwed it up for a filter, licked the papers. He twisted the far end before lighting up, took a lungful of smoke, and held it in while he passed the joint to Jimmy. 'Well, bud,' he said, exhaling. 'This time next week you'll be in uniform, all that fuckin hair cut off, standin on a parade ground. With some bastard yellin in your ear tellin you what a knob you is.'

'Reckon I will,' Jimmy agreed, passing on the sweet-smelling joint. Inhaling, Ben focused on not betraying his inexperience by coughing.

'Rather you than me,' Phil said. 'Tell you what, if I had to go in the army, not that I would, like, but if we was invaded by Russkies, you know what I'd be?'

'Quartermaster?' Ben offered.

'Sniper,' Phil said. 'Work alone. Behind enemy lines.'

'Only trouble with that is,' said Jimmy, 'you'd need to be a good shot.' He turned to Ben. 'Ever see anyone put so many bullets to so little use?'

Phil burped. 'You got a point there, bud,' he admitted.

Phil drank whisky, Jimmy vodka. Each passed his bottle to Ben, who took a slug and passed it back. He'd not drunk like this before, spirit neat and plentiful. Phil broke open a fresh packet of No. 6, threw the cellophane and silver paper on the embers of the fire. He took out three cigarettes and passed one to each of the others, grunting with drunken effort as he raised himself up to reach them.

'Tell you what,' he said. 'Don't know how you can stand the thought of goin back in a classroom for three year. Already done two more than I ever would.'

'Where you goin again?' Jimmy asked.

'Lancaster,' Ben told him. 'Plant biology.'

'Take no notice of that pig-ignorant sod,' Jimmy advised. 'What you forget,' he told Phil, 'is tis all paid for.'

Phil shook his head. 'Not for me, that lark, bud.'

'I'm the same as you,' Jimmy said, turning back to Ben. 'I'll come out the army fully qualified mechanic. HGVs, motorbikes, the lot. All paid for.'

Phil took a swig of whisky. 'Couldn't do it,' he said. 'Be one a the crowd. On the rifle range seven-fifteen. In the classroom eight forty-five. Eat at nine, shit at ten. Tell you when to wank, shouldn't be surprised.'

Jimmy stood up, turned round, took a couple of steps away from the campfire, and unzipped his flies.

'I'll be out in nine year,' Jimmy said over his shoulder, in the background the sound of his piss falling on the dry undergrowth. 'Open my own garage. You'll still be stuck on that pig farm on a labourer's fuckin wages. Meantime I'll have been out a here, seen the world.'

'Seen the streets a Belfast, more like,' Phil said. 'You can keep em, bud. Anyway, you'll miss this place.'

'Like fuck.' Jimmy zipped his flies, returned to his spot, took a swig from his bottle.

'No, I'm tellin you.' Phil pointed a wavering finger at his friend. 'Part a you's planted in this here land. You'll miss it.'

Jimmy laughed. 'As for Ben there, unlike us, he won't never have to get his hands dirty.'

'Seriously,' Phil said. 'Can't be all bad in the army. I dunno. Unarmed combat should be a laugh.'

Jimmy spluttered a mouthful of vodka at the fire. 'Only unarmed combat you ever do's with birds.'

Jimmy was a well-known scrapper. At village discos, outside pubs, he loved to fight with guys small and belligerent as himself. If you looked closely you could see the damage all over his young head – missing tooth, broken nose, misshapen ear.

'And I'll give you a word of advice for when I'm gone, bay,' Jimmy continued. 'Saw you give my sister-in-law that smile a yours. Wouldn't go anywhere near her. My brother'll do more 'an play practical jokes on you. Meanest fucker I know, and that includes the old man.'

The image of the young woman in Jimmy's kitchen that morning swam into Ben's blurry vision. 'God, she's pretty, though,' he blurted out.

Phil burst out laughing. 'He's the one you need a worry about, bud. Look: bay gone and fell in love at first sight.'

'Don't you go within ten fuckin mile a her,' Jimmy advised.

'Just think of they girls waitin for you in Manchester,' Phil suggested.

'Lancaster,' Ben corrected him. He wanted the conversation to track backwards. 'All I said was how pretty she is.'

'Bah!' Jimmy exclaimed. 'What's pretty got to do with it? You ever licked a quim, bay?'

Ben did not reply.

'You hear me?' Jimmy said. 'You never been down on a bird?'

'Leave him alone,' Phil said.

'Only askin,' Jimmy said. 'Just wonderin.'

Ben imagined they could see him blush in the dying light of the fire. He suspected they were staring at him, but whenever he glanced in their direction, they'd just looked away.

Ben pulled himself to his feet, and stumbled along the wide track by which they'd entered the forest. He fumbled through the gate and across the empty car park. Would his brain adapt to cannabis? Or would it always churn everything up? His sense of it was not of a dead weed but organic living matter: it infiltrated his brain cells and messed with their connections.

Reaching the water's edge, Ben peered across the long reservoir. Somewhere at that far end water overflowed, became the Teign river, heading for their own valley. Ben had always understood he had to leave this place. His life lay elsewhere. Whether or not, beyond holiday vacations, he would come back to his home county, he didn't know. Or miss it, as Phil had claimed Jimmy would.

The dope was wearing off. The reservoir, gunmetal grey, swallowed the last of the shadows of the trees. Darkness.

As soon as he woke up, Ben felt dreadful, head throbbing. He unzipped his sleeping bag and staggered stiffly to his feet. A blood-filled drum pounded in his skull. Jimmy and Phil lay on the ground, their leather jackets draped over them. The dog, curled up beside Jimmy, watched Ben pass.

Lurching along the path through the waist-high grass, Ben thought how much he'd like a large mug of tea and some rounds of crisp toast. The sky was speckled with cloud, the morning dewy and still. He remembered that he'd got up to empty his bladder and had already wandered for thirty yards. He found a space to one side. Peeing, he looked around. A little way along the path three pairs of limpid, alert eyes watched him.

Ben kept as still as he could but maybe his excitement transmitted itself: the three does turned and cantered away, bodies undulating, breasting through the high grass; their rumps showed intermittently, white circles with a black stripe.

He ran back to camp. 'They're here. I've seen them.' Phil and Jimmy began to stir, groggily. 'Get the guns. Quick.'

Ben and Pete loaded their rifles. 'Fuck,' Jimmy muttered. 'Forgot to loosen my bow.'

They sprinted along the path through the grass, bending forward as they ran, each holding his weapon horizontal in his hand. Jimmy's dog ran madly parallel, off in the trees. Ben studied the grass in the yards ahead. After two or three minutes' running he stopped, holding up his hand.

'See this,' he said. The way before them was unbroken. 'Reckon they must have headed into the trees here, up to our left. Phil, stay here. Jimmy, go fifty yards back along the path, I'll go the same further on, then we advance in a line. Try and corral the deer between us. And if you can't control the dog, tie her up, we'll come back for her later.'

Jimmy bent to his spaniel and secured her with his belt to the trunk of a sapling.

They moved up through the trees at a swift and even pace, keeping each other in intermittent sight, scanning ahead for movement. Concentrating, Ben forgot his pounding brain. They'd been tracking for an hour when they saw a great white wall through the trees up ahead. They continued forward, and came to the edge of the fir plantation. Beyond the chest-high wire fence lay Dartmoor, under a thick white cloud of fog.

Jimmy came in from the flank. 'What happened to they deer, then?' he demanded. 'Slip past us?'

Each of them peered out into the milky fog.

'What you reckon?' Jimmy asked.

'What we come for, innit?'

'How the hell we goin a find anythin out there?'

'Won't ever know till we try,' Ben suggested, climbing over the fence.

As soon as they lost sight of one another they realised the danger, called each other's names and reassembled. Thereafter they proceeded in a huddle, shivering.

Streams flowed down from the high watersheds of the moor, creating blanket bogs. Ben wondered at the variety of plants. Cotton grass with white tufts, bright green sphagnum moss, purple moor grass. Vegetation grew like mats floating on a spongey lake. The boys stepped on something not entirely solid, the ground for yards around quaking, undulating.

'Fuckin mental,' Jimmy said. 'Whoever heard a huntin in the summer anyhow? My brother was right. You hunts deer in the winter.'

'Christ!' Phil stopped with such abruptness that the other two jumped back. 'What's that?'

'Where?'

'Out there,' Phil said, peering in front of him, pointing into the mirk. 'I seen it.'

'Didn't see nothin,' Jimmy whispered, gazing ahead, carefully loading an arrow into his bow and raising it in front of him. Ben and Phil each raised his rifle, put the scope to his eye, scanned the fog. They began to take wary steps forward.

Whether the animal came towards them or the fog lifted just where it stood, the three men saw it at the same moment and let fly simultaneously. Ben's pellet struck the animal's side, Jimmy's arrow entered its rear flank, and it gave a whinny of surprise and pain. They understood what it was, but Jimmy named it anyhow as it disappeared into the fog. 'A pony. We shot a Dartmoor pony.'

'What are we goin a do?' Phil wailed. They all realised his bullet must have missed. 'Christ almighty. What'll we do now?'

No one answered. The chances of finding the animal, wandering wounded in the fog, were negligible; and what on earth would they do if they came across it? Instead they turned and ran back down to the forest. They clambered over the fence, and scrambled down between lines of trees. Back on the path, Jimmy found his dog, while Ben and Phil made for the camp. Ben rolled up his sleeping bag while Phil packed the guns away.

Panting, they loaded up, pulled the bikes out of the trees and rode along the path back to the main track out of the woods. There were three cars in the car park this Saturday mid-morning; they saw no one, though there was no guarantee that no one saw them. Once again they manoeuvred the bikes through the walkers' gate. Ben climbed back on, and Phil and Jimmy accelerated out along the lane around the reservoir.

Turning to his left, Ben perceived disturbance on the surface of the wide expanse of the reservoir. It took a moment to ascertain that a light rain pattered on the water.

What had they left behind? he wondered. A pony stumbling around on the moor with an arrow and an airgun pellet embedded in its flesh. An empty whisky bottle. Motorcycle tyre marks in the forest floor. He figured Jimmy would burn the bow before he set off for the army. As for his own air rifle, he would wipe it of fingerprints, wrap it in oilcloth. He thought of a place he knew where he might bury it.

Ben considered Phil, whose waist he clung on to as the rider opened up the throttle on these roads turning slippery with rain. He tried to anticipate the camber of the road, leaning together with Phil into the curves.

He reckoned that Phil would gamble, take a chance that no one would ever find the bullet with which he'd missed the animal; would hold on to his rifle. And then Ben concentrated fully, as he realised that Phil had entered a left-curving bend too fast: the bike was getting too close to the ground, bringing their bodies with it, even as it edged too far out, across the white line in the middle of the road, into the path of anything that might come the other way around the bend. Ben focused only on that moment, that one curve in the road down to Moretonhampstead.

His life was elsewhere. It always had been. It lay far ahead of him now.

Brothers at the Beach

'I need to see you,' I told my brother on the phone. 'We need to meet.'

'We do indeed, Si,' he said. 'I was about to call you. You're psychic. What are you up to next week?'

'We'll be on holiday,' I told him. 'Buckets and spades. Mary's got us a place right on the beach. Back in Devon. James, we need to talk.'

'I'm free,' James said. 'We'll join you there. I can't wait for you to meet Delilah.'

This was someone I'd not heard of. What had happened to the last one? Jenny? 'I'll ask Mary where it is, exactly. What, you'll find a B&B?'

'You'll love her, Si. She's unbelievable. We'll come in her camper van, park outside.'

'We're staying in a tiny place,' I protested. 'A chalet.'

'We'll sleep in the van,' James said. 'I can't wait to tell Delilah and Julian. You're right, Si. It's been far too long. A year? Two?'

'Three and a half,' I said, certain he remembered that Christmas as well as I did. And Julian, who the hell was he? I put the phone down, realising I now had to explain to Mary how the call I'd steeled myself to make to bring the bastard into line had somehow turned itself into an invitation to share our precious holiday. It was the kind of thing that happened, you saw it happening right there in front of you but you couldn't stop it. It had occurred, and reoccurred, since the day that James was born.

It was raining when we arrived. The children had squabbled inside the car; now they refused to get out.

'I knew we should have gone somewhere hot,' Mary said.

'You're the one figured we couldn't afford it,' I objected.

'A cheap Greek package,' Mary said wistfully. 'I mean, *look* at this ... shed. And we'll probably be stuck inside all week.'

I dragged our luggage into the sitting room. Mary had a point. This luxury chalet was partitioned into minute cubicles; a mini double bed wedged into one, a bunk bed squeezed into the other. My wife was the one with the full-time job: a social worker, she worked too hard; she needed a decent break.

'It's not so bad,' I said. 'And the forecasters don't always get it right. Specially in coastal areas.'

Mary hauled boxes of food into the kitchen-diner, dumped them on the table.

'Could brighten up tomorrow. You never know.'

Mary looked at me. 'Why don't you leave me to unpack?' she suggested. 'Take the children with you.'

I gazed out of the bleary window at rain bouncing on the chassis of our car, its own windows all steamed up. 'How?' I asked.

'Bribery. Ice cream. Oh, I don't know, Simon. Think of something.'

Anorak hoods on, heads down, we walked into the rain. The beach was deserted, almost, not quite. Two children skipped in the choppy shallows. An old man strolled, bent over, studying shells. Each raindrop hit the wet sand like a bullet, made its own splash amongst millions. You could just make out boats tied up in the bay, rocking furiously in the seething sea.

'I don't want an ice cream,' Ellie yelled.

'I can't hear you,' I said. The sea roared, rain poured down from the heavens.

Jack tugged my arm. He was squinting up at me, his spectacles a blurred screen. 'Hot chocolate?' he wondered.

My only sibling was two years younger than me. Our father was a GP, our mother a science teacher, and we each disappointed them in our own way. I drifted through school, happy only with a sketch pad in my hand. Through childhood, youth, I drew the world: a hundred views of the city of Exeter; trees, fields, animals along the Teign valley where we lived. At art school I was encouraged to draw what I saw inside my head. In my twenties I combined the two: colours and movement in oil on canvas, Turner my master then and always. Irregular exhibitions, sporadic sales; enough to pretend I was a serious artist. But perhaps I became one. It's what I do, it's who I am, and I don't know what's more important, inherent talent or dedicated engagement, honestly I don't.

James had similar leanings, it emerged, but in him it was in his hands as much as his mind. The beauty of objects made. Catapults, bows and arrows; go-karts; a treehouse at the bottom of our garden that grew in spurts of activity then lay neglected, mossy and rotting. He left school at sixteen; our father found a course in cabinet-making at a small place in north Devon, gave James a set of chisels with Swiss ash handles and gleaming steel. A whetstone. Oil.

My brother had a feel for wood, but he didn't stick the course, couldn't get on with the tutor. 'Wanker,' James confided in me, smiling. 'I come up with ways to do things better, he doesn't want to know.'

Dad got him an apprenticeship of sorts with a well-known furniture designer who had his own workshop near Bovey Tracey, three or four blokes working for him, commissions all over the country. James lasted six months; it wasn't clear whether he'd been asked to leave. 'Tosser,' he told me, grinning, shaking his head. 'Enjoyed having slaves follow his designs to the sodding letter. *Loved* it, Si.'

James had talent, lacked only what it took to see a job through. He lived at home for a while, and the house, and garage, began to fill with beautiful pieces of unfinished furniture. He got odd jobs as a carpenter, made no effort to disguise the fact that the work was beneath him. Lived hand to mouth, with women whose homes he moved in and out of.

Whenever I visited my parents, James was mostly what we talked about. It took a long time for them to lose their faith in him. He was always on the brink of a breakthrough, my mother believed: turning things around, coming into his own, at last. It didn't bother me that they gave him money, but he hit thirty and it never stopped, and they grew older, and he began to beg for wodges of cash to pay a month's rent, get a new vehicle, help him out of some fix.

Our parents live not far from me now, in Oxfordshire. My mother is anxious. My father, confused by lapses of memory, worries about what will be there if they need it; that he and our mother will find themselves impoverished at the end of their days. Last week I offered to look through their finances, just to reassure them. A large sum of money had recently been taken from one of their savings accounts. My father had no idea where it had gone. My mother, when I pushed her about it, finally admitted she'd given it to James.

'Oh, Simon, I had to,' she said, querulously. 'It was to pay off a debt. I dread to think what they'd have done to him.'

***

Ellie and Jack had been placated, hot chocolate followed by handfuls of silver for slot machines in an arcade. The sky cleared. Other people emerged from cafes, the cinema, small crowded shops; gathered on the seafront, gazing across the calm sea at a salmon-coloured sunset. Big ships crawled along the horizon, this way or that.

When we got back to the chalet park, there was a rusting Volkswagen camper van jammed in between our Vauxhall Mondeo and the cabin. As we sidled past the van I saw there was someone inside: a girl, with long brown hair, staring straight ahead. She was nodding to herself, steadily, as if agreeing with some internal conjecture. Suddenly she blinked, and gazed through the smeared window at me, then Ellie, then Jack. It was a boy. He had a thin, delicate face.

There was a commotion behind us. I heard my name called, and turned to find myself clasped in a meaty embrace by my brother. 'Si,' he sighed in my ear. 'It's so good to *see* you.' When eventually he allowed us to part and shifted his attention to the children, I ascertained what I'd felt, prickling: James had grown a beard. It was trimmed short, and flecked with grey, and, though his eyes sparkled impishly as ever, the beard aged him. It looked like a disguise, and it was. Whenever you'd not seen him for a while my brother always looked different – haircut, earring, glasses.

We began shuffling into the chalet. I glanced back at the boy in the van. He reached in through his long hair and pulled out two tiny earphones, and leaned towards the sliding side door.

Squashed in the kitchen with Mary was another woman, to whom James introduced me: Delilah. I put out my hand but she reached beyond such formality, planting a kiss on each of my cheeks. She was terribly pretty – as James's girlfriends always were, though it still surprised me. And she would surely turn out to be intelligent too, yet gullible, like all the others, fooled into falling for my brother.

'Thought they'd come a day early,' Mary said. She spoke as if delighted, though there was an ironic tone buried there, for my ears only.

'We found we could,' James said, grinning, 'and thought, *Why not?*'

We ate supper on our knees, pasta and pesto Mary stretched to seven, she and I eating out of cereal bowls. From glass tumblers we drank wine James had brought, two bottles of vintage claret so rich and smooth it was like drinking velvet, superior to anything I'd ever tasted in my entire life.

'Smuggled it out of Léoville a month ago,' James told us.

'They'll be after you,' Mary said, murmuring with pleasure. 'They'll want it back.'

James chuckled. 'I thought we could do with a treat.'

It was entirely typical of my brother. He would turn up skint, wearing brand-new designer clothes. He once arrived at our house on a new bicycle, unable, he said, to afford a car. I noted the make and model of the bike and looked it up on the internet: it sold for about £2,000.

How much the wine had cost I couldn't imagine. Mary caught my eye at one point and raised her glass, said, 'Cheers,' and I understood she was wondering the same thing too.

'What are you most looking forward to?' James asked Ellie.

Our daughter frowned, giving herself a moment to make sure it wasn't a trick question. 'Sailing,' she decided. 'Or windsurfing if we can find somewhere.'

'Julian likes surfing,' said Delilah.

'I'm going to find a fossil,' said Jack, opening his arms out wide. '*This* big.'

After supper James went out to the van and came back with two guitars.

'The kids probably need to get an early night,' I objected.

'No we don't!' they chorused disloyally.

James passed a guitar to Julian and they began tuning up. I couldn't look at Mary. We once found ourselves camping with James and his then girlfriend, and each evening descended into a droning sing-song around the fire. Mary or I had only to sing the one word *Guantanamera* to bring the whole awful episode back; it became part of our lexicon of private humour. The arrogance of amateur minstrels! When Delilah began singing the words to 'The Night They Drove Old Dixie Down' in a fake Southern accent and a high purity of tone that was like a tribute to Joan Baez herself, I saw we – and now our children, too – were in for another such ghastly evening.

I had to admit, however, as the trio played their way through a succession of mostly American folk songs – 'Two Soldiers', 'Solitary Man', and others I didn't recognise – that it wasn't that simple. Delilah's voice, once you accepted the cod accent, soared through the tunes. And while James just strummed the chords, I realised that not only I but Mary and our children too all had our attention drawn to the same spot: while the slender fingers of Julian's left hand pressed on the frets, those of his right hand picked notes from the strings in an intricate dance around the spine of each song. Bent over the guitar, the boy's brown hair fell in front of his face. Whether he or his mother, singing with her eyes closed, was leading the other I was not sufficiently musical to determine. Together, they entranced us. I couldn't help but hope that my feckless brother had at last found someone he might abide by.

That night it occurred to me to whisper to Mary – before she did to me – 'How long are they staying?'

'How would I know?' she whispered back.

'You were chatting with Delilah.'

'When are you going to talk with him?'

'I'll find a moment,' I said. 'Don't you worry.'

***

In the morning Ellie and Jack had already been outside and scouted around when the van's occupants funnelled into the chalet, first to take turns in the tiny bathroom – you could hardly avoid hearing what went on in there – and then to help themselves to breakfast.

The morning was glorious: blue sky, glassy sea, wheeling seagulls whose caws seemed to invite people down to the smooth sandy beach. We spent it building a sandcastle. James initiated the enterprise as soon as we'd established our position on the beach, grabbing Jack's spade and curving a great arc for the castle moat. It must have been four or five feet in diameter and in that one declarative flourish, my brother committed the entire family to hours of hard labour, interspersed with dashes into the freezing English Channel.

James worked furiously. We brothers had twin physiques: big-boned, barrel-chested. I'd guess we both weighed within a pound or two of fourteen stone. Back to back, armed with a spade each, we gouged out the moat until we met up around the other side. Then we criss-crossed the castle compound with internal gullies, leaving four segments, platforms on which we adults could each unleash our sandy creativity. James went for bulk, and volume, amassing material; Mary began building a pyramid of damp sand; Delilah collected shells and seaweed.

While we worked, Ellie fell laughing off her bodyboard in the gentle waves; Jack let Julian tow him, running silently through the shallows. Occasionally one or other would visit us like some juvenile Pharaoh checking up on their slaves' progress, adding a decorative pebble before running back to the water.

Without consciously intending to, I found myself competing with my brother: at two opposite corners of the castle rose towers. James's grew ever higher, a great obelisk; while mine, once it reached about four feet, I began to crenellate. Our children were delighted. Mary and Delilah found common ground in decrying the blatant symbolism of their men's infantile contest — though there was an edge of derision in Mary's voice, where in Delilah's I heard only flirtatious affection. This reminded me of the nature of my brother's inconstancy: when that playful tone in the voice of his woman faded, he'd leave her.

On the crowded beach passers-by tarried to appreciate our citadel. Children stood and stared. James recruited them: half a dozen little navvies joined Julian, Ellie and Jack digging a long runnel down the beach to the shoreline, ready for the incoming tide. They all looked like they were copying my brother, backs bent, shovelling sand with their hands, sweating.

Along the promenade people wandered behind perky dogs on long leads, and ate ice creams. An old couple sat in a pair of deckchairs, dressed in winter clothes. The crowd jostled to and fro. Small sports events sprang up around us: stout women played beach ping-pong; men with muscled legs chased Frisbees, bellies wobbling. Their beautiful offspring frolicked in the water. You might infer from the scene that there was human progress, one generation to the next, ugly couples producing miraculous children, if you didn't know that puberty would come and twist them into their parents.

James's architectural ambition had, it became gradually clear, committed us not only to a long morning's construction but the afternoon too, for how could we abandon our fortress without witnessing its surrender to the ocean's assault? The women returned to the chalet to collect lunch, I rubbed dry my shivering children, applied suncream to their reddening shoulders. Julian gleaned sticks of driftwood.

We munched sandwiches, crunched apples. Out in the bay, small dinghies with single sails – blue, red and yellow triangles – scurried from side to side. Manned by teenagers in wetsuits and orange life jackets, they tacked and turned about. I've never found conflict easy. Whenever our parents argued I left the house. My brother and I rarely fought; when we did I was brought to tears more often than he. Mary and I merely bicker, and she disciplines our children. But I knew I couldn't let things go on as they were.

'James,' I said. 'Let's find a cafe, you and me.'

'Wait,' he said, launching himself to his feet. 'Hang on, Si. Had an idea.' He strode off between picnicking families to the back of the beach, hopped over the low stone wall on to the busy promenade, and disappeared.

Julian beat his driftwood drumsticks on stones he'd grouped in a small semicircle. It was less a performance than a private experiment, but Ellie and Jack watched, spellbound, while Mary and I tidied up the remnants of lunch. Delilah lit a pink Sobranie. Between elegant puffs she held the cigarette aloft, as if doing so with style was obligatory.

James reappeared with a multicoloured pack of felt-tip pens. 'We need stones,' he told the children. 'Smooth and pale as you can find.'

Needless to say, we all became involved, drawing faces and flowers and patterned designs in a familial burst of visual flair. We pressed the coloured stones into the walls and turrets of our sandcastle, as the tide made its sly approach. The beach below us thinned out; children playing in the shallows came closer. People traipsed away, heavy-laden, for the long climb up to the car parks.

By the time an advance party of seawater flowed into the moat, our citadel, with its eccentric quartet of towers, was the most finely adorned in Christendom. Mary took photos on her mobile, members of the construction gang kneeling proudly around. Ruination followed, surprisingly rapid, and we watched with that fascination destruction offers the human soul. Once the moat filled up and the walls were breached, the towers, undermined, soon subsided, and the brightly coloured stones sank beneath wet sand.

A fish and chip supper was voted for and we joined a queue at a place whose aroma of fish and vinegar and deep-frying fat enticed us.

'You pay for this, Si,' James suggested. 'De and I'll go get some wine. Catch you at the chalet.' Delilah whispered something to Julian, he nodded, and she and James went off.

'Nothing too expensive,' I called out. He raised an arm in dismissive acknowledgement. After twenty or thirty yards he and Delilah reached towards each other, and their fingers entwined.

It was dusk. We'd long since consumed our supper, washed down with water, when the lovers returned. They made no apology for having been gone more than two hours. On the contrary, they seemed mightily pleased with themselves, as they handed me two bottles of supermarket plonk. 'Two for the price of one,' Delilah announced, and I calculated that our disjointed dinner had cost me £35, my brother a fiver. Nor did they seem bothered by the extent to which their meal, kept warm in the oven, had dried out. Rather, they hymned the delights of the brittle chips and crusty batter, pantomiming for the benefit of our children, who watched them closely. James stuck a chip in each nostril: Jack hooted. Delilah pretended to be Chinese, a pair of thin chips becoming chopsticks with which she struggled to eat others, and I could see our ten-year-old Ellie noting a role model's every movement.

It struck me with instant certainty that James and Delilah had somehow had sex somewhere during their wine-buying interlude.

At least they retired, with the silent Julian, to their camper van and let us all turn in at a decent hour, our eyelids droopy, our bodies weighted down with the beautiful exhaustion that comes from the ocean air.

The following morning Mary suggested a visit to the fossil museum.

'I'd rather head straight out and look for our own,' James said.

'So would I!' exclaimed both Ellie and Jack.

'Might it be an idea,' I wondered, 'to learn what to look for first?'

'You can tell us if we're doing it wrong,' James declared. 'Can't he, kids? I've got a hammer in the van. Basically, you just break stones open.'

Agreeing to meet back at the chalet at noon, Mary and I watched the others cross the pebbled beach towards the fossil cliffs. Delilah held Ellie's hand. Seven-year-old Jack walked beside Julian, every few yards glancing up at him, as if worried the older boy might open his mouth and say something, and Jack miss it. My brother strode in front, leading the way like some Pied Piper in his cut-off jeans and sandals.

'Do you think they'll be all right?' Mary asked.

'Of course they will,' I assured her, rather wishing someone would do the same for me. We strolled away from the chalet park past the beach and along the promenade into the small town, in whose steep high street we discovered three charity shops and one bona fide second-hand bookshop, in each of which we rummaged companionably. I bought a thriller. Mary found a T-shirt for Jack and a cap she thought Ellie might like. We then spent an hour in the museum, during which we discovered that our fossil hunters had headed in the wrong direction: richer pickings were to be found east rather than west of the town. Even though it meant that my children would have suffered as a result of my brother's ignorant spontaneity, this information gave me, I confess, a certain mean-minded pleasure.

As Mary and I headed back to the chalet, laden with fresh supplies from the supermarket, she paused to kiss me. My mind was stirred with amorous intention, but the others were there already, on the cramped verandah to the seaward side of the cabin. On the table was a pile of sticks. Apart from Delilah, who I could see through the window in the kitchen, from where there came an enticing smell of chocolate, everyone sat in plastic chairs, bent over; they were whittling pieces of driftwood, with an assortment of knives.

Noting my presence, James said, 'Not an ammonite in sight. The whole place has been picked clean.'

'Look, Daddy,' Ellie said, holding up the stick she seemed to be carving into a kind of mini totem pole. 'I'm going to colour it later, too.'

Jack was sharpening a sliver of wood to a fine point. Mary came round the side of the chalet behind me, saw the knife our boy was proudly wielding, and shrieked. Each whittler jumped. Jack stared at his thumb – as too, over the next few seconds, did everyone else. At first we did so because that was where Mary was looking, but the particular way in which Jack sat rigid, horror-struck by something he knew had happened but was yet unfelt and unseen, gripped my attention. Then it appeared, a scarlet line of blood rising out of the cut in his thumb. Jack started sobbing, Mary was beside him, a tissue unearthed from her pocket.

'Plaster,' she said, and I rushed to the car and grabbed the green medical bag.

The cut was not deep. Once he had a plaster on, badge of pain and bravery, Jack began to recover himself. Mary, though, was shaking her head. No one spoke, waiting while she packed away the first aid. Finally, she let it out.

'I cannot be*lieve* you gave a sharp knife to a seven-year-old child,' she said, addressing my brother without looking at him. As if to emphasise the point, she picked up the penknife and warily closed it.

James, fortunately, said nothing. Instead, our own daughter spoke up to defend him. 'Jack was fine till you yelled, Mummy.'

'And his girlfriend,' Mary continued, transferring James from second to third person, and thereby, I understood, dragging me into it, 'is in my kitchen, where she's taken our various chocolate bars from the fridge and melted them together in a saucepan.'

The gravity of this second charge, articulated in the open air, made me want to giggle. If someone else had, it would quite likely have set us all off. There was instead a fearful silence.

'Who'd like to help me get lunch together?' I asked, eventually. 'We can eat out here.' Ellie rose to assist, and followed me inside.

'Pass stuff out the window,' James called.

Mary sat with her wounded son on her lap, hugging him close to her. Julian raised the stick he'd been whittling to his lips and blew. A breathy squeak emerged. He was carving a whistle.

We ate lunch in a tense atmosphere that was no aid to digestion. Dessert consisted of what Delilah presented as 'chocolate sludges', reconstituted blobs of the melted chocolate bars, and they were strangely delectable, laying traces of their parentage on one's tongue. Delilah ate none herself, but leaned back with one of her coloured cigarettes. The day was hot and snoozy, the sea blue-grey, calm and inviting: there was a general consensus, led by the children, to return to the beach. In the commotion of clearing the table I drew my brother aside.

'Can we talk now?' I asked him. 'Let's you and me take a stroll, join the others in a while.'

'Thanks, Si,' James said. 'I appreciate it. It needn't take long. I just have to get some things off my chest, you know?'

He stood up and started gathering cutlery. What on earth was he talking about? 'No. No, I'm the one who wants to talk, James,' I insisted, but my brother had already turned away, passing a tray of cheese and hummus back through the window.

We walked off as they had done earlier, west along the shore, our feet crunching on pebbles in the hot sun. While the sandy beach behind us was jam-packed, along this stretch were scattered less gregarious families. They lay uncomfortably on rugs which were landscapes of miniature undulation, and tiptoed down the steep shelf to the sea.

'Lovely girlfriend,' I said.

'Delilah?' he asked, as if there were someone else I should have noticed. 'Yeh. Thanks. She's okay.'

'And Julian,' I said. 'Some musician. When he plays that guitar it's hard to believe the boy's only thirteen.'

James grinned. 'Ah, it's only talent, Si, eh?'

I realised that my brother was mocking me, but whether he was implying that I myself had too little talent, or that I made the opposite mistake of putting too much emphasis on it, I couldn't tell. We walked beyond the last swimmers. Dotted here and there ahead of us were people on their knees, poking about in the debris that had fallen from the grey cliffs.

'About the knife,' James said. 'Sorry, Si. But Ellie was right. I mean, you and I got up to a lot worse when we were kids.'

As he said this James made a slight nod, in a vague westerly direction, up and over the cliffs towards the middle of Devon.

'You thinking of looking in on old haunts?' I asked him.

James stopped walking. 'No,' he said. 'But now you mention it.'

'It was just the way you … ' I mumbled. 'I thought … '

'The two of us. Yes, Si. What, you and me drive over there tomorrow? See if any of the old faces are around.'

'We could take the others,' I ruminated. 'Show them where we come from.'

'Either way,' James concurred, 'it's a great idea. Ah, to hell with it. Let's get back to the gang.'

My brother took my arm, and gently turned me right around.

'I wanted to have words with you,' James said. 'But now I feel like we're reconnected, Si.' He smiled at me, his blue eyes glinting in the sun. It was easy enough to see how girls had always fallen for him. He'd perfected that smile at the age of fourteen. It was a cheap trick and it wasn't going to work on me.

'No, James,' I said. '*I* need to talk with *you*. And if there's something on your mind too, by all means share it.'

James strolled head down, pondering this request. We began passing those we'd passed earlier. An elderly couple emerged from the water, climbing the pebbled shore, a pair of ageing wrinkled nymphs.

My brother took a deep breath. 'Okay,' he said. 'Fair enough, Si. What it is is this: all my life I've had you looking down on me. I'm not prepared to put up with it any longer. You've chosen your way of life: marriage to

a solid, wage-earning woman, two well-behaved children, house in suburbia, security, caution. I respect that.
It's your choice. It's not mine. I don't want to settle ...
down, give up my freedom.'

It seemed my brother had rehearsed a litany of his
resentment – as, of course, had I. We walked slowly
and fell into step, crunching on the pebbles. The way
he made our children being well-behaved a part of his
contempt did something to my heart: I felt a thud of my
pulse, the temperature of my blood rise.

'What have I ever done to hurt you, Si?' James
continued. 'Yet I can feel you and your wife's disap-
proval every time I see you. Why do you think I never
drop in on you when I visit the old folks? I mean, let's
be honest, Mary's always had a problem with me.'

Damned right she has, I thought. 'I just think,' I said,
'she works with clients who lead chaotic lives, and lack the
resources to do things differently. Whereas you don't.'

James stopped again. 'Exactly!' he said. 'I knew
it.' He shook his head, grinning. 'Don't you see, our
choices are personal. One is not better than the other.
I'm forty-two years old, and I'm not prepared any
longer to be looked down on, by anyone, least of all my
older fucking brother.'

We passed the chalet park, which seemed strangely
deserted, and the sailing club, single-masted yachts
parked up on the concrete. I could feel a burning in my
chest. 'I'm two years older than you, James,' I told him.
'I can't *help* looking down on you.'

'Don't be so fucking puerile,' James said. 'Concealing your anger, as ever. You wanted to have it out and now you're trying to sidle away.'

'Well, all right,' I said, 'you've got a point. I *do* think of you as my kid brother. And I'll start treating you as a mature adult the day you stop scrounging money off our ageing parents.'

'Oh, *that*,' James said, dismissing it with a wave of his hand. 'What's that to you?'

'What's it to *me*?' I gasped. 'Have you no idea how anxious Mum is about money? Council tax, energy bills, food bills, everything goes up, their pensions stay the same, she has her own small nest egg which you're burrowing into like some unpleasant natural phenomenon, a parasitic offspring; the BBC Wildlife Unit should make a programme about children like you.'

'Oh, very good, Si,' James said. 'Very funny.' He turned towards me, frowning. 'It's not about them, is it? They've not lent me very much, actually.'

'Lent? Is that what you call it? What, you're going to pay them back?'

We were now in amongst people, though I was not aware of them except as vague coloured shapes we passed through, across the promenade.

'No,' James said. 'You think I'm taking what's yours. Well, don't worry, Si. You can tell Mary not to worry, either. I'm only taking an advance on my *own* inheritance. Not yours.'

We walked along the crowded sandy beach, close to the water. I didn't see the others up ahead of us – in fact

I don't think I could see anything at all in that moment, my vision was a red blur, there was only my body lumbering blindly forward – but Mary tells me she saw us, bobbing or shaking our heads.

'How dare you?' I said. 'How fucking *dare* you? You filch money off Mum and Dad and accuse *me* of worrying about *my* money? You little shit, James.'

My brother smiled. 'Hit a tender spot, eh, Si, old boy? Still bothered by living off the wife, I suppose. You're an artist, Si, you're *supposed* to live off people. They *like* it. It makes the Marys of this world feel *useful*. But I guess you figured that your inheritance would pay her back.'

The heat had risen and now my head was on fire, my skull melting, other shapes could have been forming from it. 'I have no plans,' I said, my voice all out of control, 'to take anything from our parents.'

'You see, the difference between us,' James said, 'is you always needed Mummy and Daddy's approval, I never did, and you know what? You *still* do.'

I bent and took James around the waist and with a great roar, half-lifting him, lunged sideways into the water. He was hopping on one leg backwards through the shallows. Mary said it must have looked highly comical to those who did not know me, two large, fully clothed, middle-aged men larking about. As we plunged beyond knee-high depth, the water slowed our momentum. We spun together and fell with a huge splash. Children who had scattered now stood back and watched us, in a widening radius of attention.

I punched my brother. He landed blows on my head. It felt as if we had three or four arms each, grabbing and hitting each other, flailing with unpractised fists. I felt my head go under the water, then out again. There was salt and blood in my mouth.

Somehow James was managing not only to attack me from in front but also to pull me off him. Then I realised that these were the hands of other men, dragging me away from my brother. My sight was restored to me and I saw that men hauled him back too, and I could hear the screaming voices of women.

I was out of breath and gasping. 'Thank you,' I said, to those who had restrained me. 'Thank you.' They loosened their grip. I did not yet feel the pain in my jaw, or swelling eye.

I understood at once how pathetic we must have been, what a disgraceful spectacle we'd provided. Was I ashamed? No, I felt a sense of glory coursing through my veins; understood already that this was one of the most vivid moments of my quiet life.

Delilah and Julian helped James, bedraggled, back to their camper van, and the long drive home.

I stayed on the beach, wrapped in towels, sodden clothes drying out in the hot sun. Our children sat close by, and watched me, until they'd got over the sight of their father floundering in the sea, and they wandered back down to the water themselves. Mary let me lie then with my head in her lap, and with great tenderness stroked my hair as my left eye swelled and closed.

'So,' she said, in a teasing tone of voice that was tinged with affection, 'you really told him.'

'Yes,' I said. It hurt to talk, my jaw aching. 'And nothing will change. Ever. We're stuck with it. It's just the way that it is.'

I could hear all around me the high excited voices of the crowd; then another sound, that of waves rustling on the shore. The heat of the day dissipating. People packing up. A sudden squawling chorus of seagulls, neither mocking nor applauding me. Mary joined the children, and I watched them. They waded out, to where the waves were cresting. Ellie plunged beneath the surface. Mary lifted Jack above each breaking wave, lifting him up, lifting him, up, forever.

Rapture

Jim scanned the warehouse for a sign of his daughter.

'Look away,' Doug's mum said. 'They're more likely to hurt themselves if you're watching them.'

The trouble was, Doug's mum had no idea how clumsy Lily was. Jim swept the three-storeyed, multi-coloured scaffolding of the indoor play arena. Where *was* Lily? Jim spotted Doug: the little fellow rolled, Jim saw him fall over and come straight back upright, he was like one of those roly poly toys; those wobbly men. Invulnerable. Lily was not. At home, she regularly tripped herself up, knocked elbows or knees; her face was rarely unblemished by bruises. The scaffolding poles here were wrapped in some kind of foamy polystyrene, but Jim didn't trust it.

'They know when you're watching, they check,' said Doug's mum. 'Leave them. They look after themselves.'

Were all children the same to her, diminutive blobs? She and Jim sat on yellow plastic chairs at a red table, under high, garish lights. Fred, his infant son, was asleep in his buggy beside them. In the play arena Jim saw a toddler tumble down a ramp. At the bottom she looked around on all fours with an expression of shock. He thought she was going to cry, but then a kind of manic grin spread across her features and she crawled back up the slide for another go.

'Fancy a coffee?' Doug's mum asked. 'I'll get the kids something.'

'Thanks, sure. Lily doesn't like—'

'They eat anything if they're hungry,' Doug's mum said, and, pulling her bulging woman's purse from a rucksack, pushed between chairs towards the cafe counter. Jim turned his attention back to the play arena. There was a wire mesh around the outside. Was it securely tied to the poles? Was it strong enough to withstand a small, stocky girl ricocheting against it? Scaffolding can fall away from houses, there was an incident reported in the local newspaper. A builder was killed. When was the last time this whole play frame was tested?

He spotted Lily, clambering into an orange tunnel. He watched the other end, waited for her to emerge. She didn't. She'd got stuck. The poor girl couldn't move. Panic would set in. Hysteria. She wouldn't be able to breathe, and— Wait a minute, were those her green socks appearing from the end she'd entered? Lily was reversing her way out.

Lily reminded Jim of his younger sister, the year she started at the school he already attended. Beth was a large, clumsy, deep-voiced girl who made other children laugh. She said things and people chuckled; she hopped or skipped, and they fell about, Beth wasn't entirely sure why. Her fame spread through the school, as certain children's does. 'That funny kid in Year One's your sister, Jimbo?' There was something intrinsically amusing about her, how she occupied the bodily space allotted to her in the world, and it was beyond her control. Beth sometimes felt, she would tell Jim later, as if she were someone else's comic creation. God's, perhaps.

Beth remained popular, a person who leavened with humour the air of the rooms she entered. She got jobs easily, became a valued colleague. Was now the wife of a happy man, mother of jovial children. Perhaps Lily would follow the same path.

'Here you go.' Doug's mum put a white Styrofoam cup on the table in front of him. She nodded to the boy in his buggy. 'You don't want to let them sleep in the daytime,' she said. 'They'll be up all night and then you're fucked.' She put tiny sachets of sugar and containers of milk by his cup, along with a spindly plastic twirler, or whisk. 'They don't need as much sleep as people think.'

Jim suspected Doug's mum had taken pity on him, the father on both drop-off *and* pick-up duty. 'I'm going to Kidzone if you want to come,' she'd said. 'A bit of rough'n'tumble's good for them after nursery.'

Jim took a swallow of coffee, and spat it back into the cup. 'Jesus Christ,' he said.

Doug's mum jumped. 'What is it?' she asked.

Jim grimaced. A taste of drains remained on his tongue. His mouth felt unclean. 'They call this coffee?' he said.

'Cappuccino,' Doug's mum said. 'You're welcome.'

'No, no,' he said. 'Thank you. I mean, really, thanks, it's just, you know.'

'Know what?'

'Have you tasted it? It's, like, it's shit. I mean, how can that be? Capitalism's meant to be efficient, right? And there are espresso machines out there that make *amazing* coffee. So how can a company that makes crap like this survive in the marketplace?'

Doug's mum took a sip of hers. 'Not too bad,' she said. 'I've had worse.'

'If a company making coffee this bad can prosper, what's the point? Why not have a planned economy and ... what d'you say? You've had *worse?*'

'I didn't say it was great,' Doug's mum said. 'What do you expect in a place like this? Use your eyes. It's not exactly Pret A Manger, is it?' He'd upset her. What a tosspot he was. She'd taken offence. She stood, and picked up his cup. 'I'll take it back and complain for you,' she said.

'No,' he said. 'I mean, I can do it.'

'I think you probably can't,' she said, and was away. Jim looked around. He was the only male in the entire place over the age of four. Maybe the weird taste in the coffee had been caused by a chemical reaction between caffeine and oestrogen. Having a baby was a good way to meet women; he should have thought of it much earlier in his life. If he was the kind of man turned on by lactating, postnatal women. No doubt some men were.

He'd dropped Lily at nursery that morning and driven to the park. The dogs had yapped with excitement while he got Fred out of his car seat and into the buggy. When he let them out the cocker nearly knocked the buggy over and the springer almost jerked him off his feet in her eagerness to run free. He pushed the buggy while the dogs pulled him, out of the car park. On the grass he let them off their leads. The buggy was a three-wheeler Sarah had ordered for him. 'You can run with it,' she said. 'It'll keep you fit. Help you get rid of that.' 'That' being his paunch, the result of being unable to let children's leftover food go to waste. He called it thrift. Others called it greed. He was probably one of those roly-poly toys himself now. Push him over and he'd roll upright.

He jogged past the football pitches but had to keep stopping: the dogs crapped twice each. Thankfully he'd remembered to bring a roll of black plastic poo bags with him. He used four, tied up and deposited in the red bins scattered around the park. Fred slept; back at the car he woke up. The dogs were energised by their exercise, and barked in the back while he changed Fred's nappy on the rear seat. What had possessed them to get puppies at the same time as their babies were born? Jim had a vague memory that it was his idea. He strapped Fred in the baby seat, then sat behind the wheel and closed his eyes. The sun was trying to shine. His mind was empty for a lovely moment. Then he opened his eyes and switched on the ignition.

Supermarket trolleys with a little wire seat for the baby just in front of the handle, now there was a brilliant invention! Jim pushed Fred through the fruit and veg section. He hoped the inventor had patented his or her design and got something for it for every shopping trolley in every supermarket in the world. A penny, a cent. He wouldn't begrudge that genius his or her millions. Fred reached towards black grapes and Jim plucked a cluster for him. Jamie Oliver wrote in one of his cookery books that he'd never buy fruit without tasting it: if anyone challenged Jim on this, he had his cookery guru as an alibi.

They rolled along the aisles. Jim felt for the shopping list in his back pocket. It wasn't there. What an idiot. It must be in the car; or still on the kitchen table at home. He could probably remember everything. Toilet paper, kitchen roll, washing powder. Pasta, rice, the staples. Oh, and those little sausages Lily likes. Rice cakes: they look like polystyrene and taste like it too. When Fred or Lily left fragments uneaten, he threw them in the bin. He had standards, however low. Where were the damned things? They used to be next to the Ryvita.

'Jimbo!'

He looked up. A thin man carrying a shopping basket stood before him. He knew this man.

'How's it going, Jim? You've got a kid?'

The man was a similar age to him but his clothes fitted him well, his hair was recently cut. 'Two, actually, mate, the other one's at nursery.'

'Cool.' The guy smiled. He looked like a slightly older yet sharper version of Matt Blake, an old friend he'd not seen in years. They used to go clubbing together, half a dozen of them. 'Still get to go out much?' the man asked. It *was* Matt Blake, of course!

'Much?' Jim replied. 'You mean ever? No. You?'

'Sure,' Matt said. 'Sometimes. Not as often as we used to. I'm more into sailing these days.'

'Sailing?'

'A few of us share a boat. Moored in Portsmouth. I go out most weekends.'

'Wow.'

'You'll have to come out on the Solent with us some time,' Matt said.

'Yes, great, I'd love to. Thanks, that would be brilliant.'

'Well, keep in touch.'

'You too, Matt.' Jim glanced down at Matt's basket. Bottle of wine. Cellophane-wrapped steak. Four apples in a punnet. A small carton of milk. 'Hey,' Jim said. 'We had the best times, didn't we?'

'Sure did, Jimbo,' Matt said, as they glided past each other along the aisle.

***

Jim loaded the shopping bags on to the back seat of the car. The dogs were in the boot, blessedly content there. Then he pushed the trolley to the cash machine. He'd taken Fred out of the seat and put him in the empty bed of the trolley: the infant stood up, grasping the stiff wire with his little fingers, smiling in a confused way as they rattled over the tarmac, then sat down again.

There was money available, as he trusted there would be. Sarah earned it and organised it. She'd gone back to work after just six weeks' maternity leave for both children and Jim had taken over their care. His earnings were sporadic, unpredictable. He'd always been self-employed. The mere consideration of a proper job, an employer, fixed hours, caused him palpitations and shortness of breath. He put the five £20 notes in his wallet and pushed the trolley away from the machine. As he turned, he saw the guy waiting in line behind him was wearing one of those employee tags around his neck. A badge of slavery. And the fool wasn't even at work. He was *proud* of his chains!

Jim bought and sold. He'd had a market stall; he used the internet. Books, antiques, anything really. Everyone knew him: Jim, know someone who'd be interested in this painting? Jim, what's the best way to sell my old man's car? Jimbo, how much do you think these vinyl records are worth? He could value any old piece of tat, he knew the price of things. He still didn't quite understand how he'd failed to turn much profit from this knowledge, those contacts. Laziness, partly, he'd admit to that. Lack of what some people called ambition; what he considered avarice. Not to mention a business plan. Plus people were always letting him down, messing him around. He fell out with them.

Sarah was steady. She loved work: going to an office, liaising with people, giving presentations, leading her team. She was offered promotions and accepted them.

'They said there's nothing wrong with it but they've done you another one anyway.' Doug's mum put the newly frothed, so-called cappuccino, on the red tabletop.

'Thanks,' Jim said. He sniffed, then sipped it. It was slightly less cloacal than before.

'What's your partner do, then?' Doug's mum asked.

'Wife,' Jim said, and regretted it. 'She works in the university.'

'She's an academic?'

'Admin. Policy unit.'

Doug's mum frowned. 'Policy?'

There was a certain clever curiosity suggested by her cross-questioning. Doug's mum wasn't so bad-looking. Why did intelligence in a woman quicken Jim's blood? There must be a biological explanation. It held out the promise of quick-witted lovemaking, maybe. A sudden terrifying thought struck him: did Doug's mum fancy him? Had she invited him here on some kind of *date*? Women on the make always ask men about their partners, don't they? Everyone knows that. Get men bemoaning their lot, then seduce them with sympathy.

'Yes,' he said. 'Like, climate change policy.'

'In the university?'

'Yes, like, how should the institution respond? What challenges will climate change present?'

'To students?' Doug's mum smiled. 'To tutors?'

The woman was relentless. 'Yeh, kind of what systems need to be in place to deal with it. You know?'

Doug's mum shook her head. Unbelievable. She clearly thought – just because he wasn't articulating it very well – that he didn't know what his wife did. Except that it was true. He didn't have a clue, not really. Sarah must have explained it to him. He'd been there when she explained it to others. What a twat. He looked around for Lily. He could see no sign of her.

'How about you?' he asked.

'Me?' Doug's mum said. 'Have you seen these women with kids and full-time jobs? Up early, back late. Work flat out, dash home, time with the kids, do the house-work. They're fucked.' She picked up her plastic cup and drained whatever dross was left in it. 'I've got two older ones as well.'

'At school?'

'Yeh. Secondary. Different fathers, see?'

'Okay.'

'I'm on my own again now. Which is a *lot* fucking better, I can assure you.' Doug's mum curled her upper lip. 'You can't rely on them.'

'Right,' Jim said.

'They let you down in the end.' She made a sort of chuckling, or rather snorting, sound. 'If not sooner.'

It took Jim a moment to appreciate that Doug's mum's collective *they* and *them* no longer denoted kids but now referred to men. Yet who was she addressing? Jim! He was sitting right in front of her! Not only did she not fancy him, she hadn't even registered him as a male of the species.

'Dougie!' Doug's mum yelled suddenly in the direction of the play arena. 'Leave him, Dougie!' she screamed, jumping up. Jim looked towards where she was heading and saw her son and another boy wrestling. Two little Toby Jug boys grappling. His daughter had been invited to play with a thug. At least he wasn't fighting with her.

Jim looked down at Fred. The boy had woken. He had a strange expression on his face: his eyes were glazed, his lips were soft, and pursed. He appeared to be in some kind of ecstasy; a dopey trance. It struck Jim that he had seen that expression before. He fell back through time, into another warehouse years ago. Dark, with spooling, strobing, multicoloured lights. They'd been dancing for hours, the usual group of them. He went off looking for somewhere to smoke, found Matt sitting on metal stairs outside. He looked like he was dozing. A grey dawn was breaking. He touched Matt's shoulder. Matt opened his eyes. He had that same glazed, enraptured look. They'd smiled at each other. No words were needed, or would suffice: this was happiness.

And it really was. Jim thought he'd do it for the rest of his life. How life surprised you. The idea of staying up all night, with children to look after the next day, was laughable. Sleep became the most precious commodity in creation. How sad was that?

A familiar smell entered Jim's nostrils. The expression on Fred's face was caused by the infant rapture of emptying his bowels; deliciously squeezing babyish ordure out of his arse. Jim rootled through the changing bag for a nappy and wipes, and carried his boy to the toilets. To his surprise the disabled one was clean and had a wide and sturdy changing shelf. He changed Fred's nappy, then realised that he himself needed to pee. He couldn't leave Fred lying on the shelf on the other side of the room, the boy might roll off.

What Jim knew he should do was take Fred back out and leave him with Doug's mum for a moment, come back for a quick piss on his own. So why wasn't he doing so? Why was he unbuttoning his trousers and yanking them down with one hand while hugging Fred to him with the other? The fact was he didn't trust her, did he? That was the truth. He didn't want to leave his little boy with Doug's mum for *two minutes*. What was *wrong* with him?

Men were too soft to be good parents, weren't they? Jim remembered his own mother: the sharp smacks, the clarity. He sat Fred on one thigh while he peed sitting down. Fred tried to grab a long cord: an alarm bell for disabled users. Jim batted it out of Fred's reach. He finished and stood up. It was more difficult to pull his pants and trousers up with one hand than it had been to shovel them down: he had to bend his legs so that the trousers didn't slide straight back to his ankles when he let go. Fred started kicking and grizzling. The operation was untidy, but he managed it eventually and left the toilet.

Back out in the warehouse, Doug's mum was at their table along with her boy, who was crying. Screaming, actually. Was the little hooligan upset by her scolding him before he could beat up the other kid? Had she given him a quick slap?

Jim put Fred back in his buggy, and secured the straps. He scanned the play arena. There was no sign of Lily. He'd not actually seen her, he admitted, for about ten minutes. A hot shameful flush coursed through him. Words of justification spilled from his brain. *I couldn't see ... she wouldn't stop talking ... the coffee ... the toilet ... I tried ...*

'Can you keep an eye on him?' he asked Doug's mum, and without waiting for an answer jogged towards the scaffolding. He hurled himself into the castellated entry and, bent double, barrelled past children not his own. The entire framework was partitioned into rooms, more or less, leading one to another. The temperature was ten degrees higher than outside. Ladders and slides connected each floor to the one above or below. He scrambled up and down them, an awkward giant in a maze. It was much bigger than he'd realised. He crawled into a space with tiny bumper cars like a minimal-contact dodgems. The drivers screeched and shrieked. Another room had huge bouncy exercise balls that children were shoving with all their might against other children they did not know. They yelled martial cries as they did so. Two black boys seemed to be trying to squash an Asian boy in an exercise-ball sandwich. The boy was winded by each cushioned thump.

Jim peered into every tunnel. He climbed to the top floor and back down, entering on all fours rooms he'd already been through, growing ever hotter and more desperate. He asked children if they'd seen her. They looked at him with dumb suspicion. What was this sweating adult doing in their realm?

Eventually he crawled through an opening and came, panting, to a new room on the ground floor in a far corner that he'd not been to before. A child left as he entered. The room was full of hundreds of different-coloured globes, each the size of a cricket ball. It was empty of children now, and though all their raucous noise was only just behind and above him, the room of balls was like a quiet pond. He understood that his daughter was in there, beneath its placid surface.

Jim dived in. The pond was not deep, and finding himself able to stand he staggered around, making great sweeps of the light balls with his hands and arms. In order to reach right to the ground he had to bend his head under the surface, among the balls, and caught himself taking deep breaths, absurdly, before plunging in. He could not find her. Had he reached right into the corners? He began again, methodically, working his way around the outside of the weird room. Then it happened. He felt something different. A clothed limb. A foot. He dived down and put his arms under the child's dumpy body and brought it up to the surface and out of the pond of hollow balls. It was Lily, all right. Her eyes were closed. Her body was limp. She had drowned. Here, in this infernal place.

But as he lifted her higher, Lily opened her eyes. A little sleepily, she looked up at her father, and smiled. The panic that had surged in his veins, the desperate stifling heat as he searched for her, were replaced by a cool breeze of relief that blew through him like some drug of the future, subtly, sweetly overwhelming.

Jim smiled back, and then he hugged his daughter tight to his paunchy torso, and let himself, let the two of them, swoon backwards into the multicoloured pond.

Generation to Generation

When we were children, we knew that the Queen had someone to sit on, and thus warm, her toilet seat before she used it.

I've no idea how we knew this. Maybe it was common knowledge, and one of us overheard an adult mention it. Or perhaps our eldest brother Benny made it up. But even so, when you think about it, it works on so many levels. You picture the act itself, this minion lowering his or her drawers and sitting on the royal throne, not to fulfil the toilet's sole function (in fact that is the one thing they must not do, isn't it? It's probably a treasonable offence, they could be sent to the Tower), but to impart the body heat of their buttocks to the wooden seat so that Her Royal Highness's buttocks should not have to suffer that brief chill familiar to us all.

You picture the minion pulling up their drawers and scurrying away just before the Queen's arrival. You imagine that Her Royal Highness would not want to pass this lackey, for in doing so she would have, however fleetingly, to acknowledge (if only to herself) what they had just done, and why. Queen Elizabeth the Second would surely prefer not to think about it at all. So this minion would scuttle away, perhaps through some secret back passage. (Yes, that's pretty funny, I agree, it just came to me.)

So you're picturing, also, the strange psychological arena that is the mind of a monarch, and indeed of those around her.

You picture too a world of class, of privilege, passed on generation to generation, a tradition of finely graded social layers and positions and functions, so to speak. At the top is the Queen. Somewhere at the bottom (ha, ha) is the royal toilet-seat warmer.

And, of course (perhaps above all), you're reminded that the Queen, just like every single one of her subjects, is a prisoner of her body, a human animal, and needs to take a daily crap.

My wife, Alli, works one day a week at the Animal Sanctuary shop. I say 'works' but she's a volunteer, unpaid. A few months ago we were talking and she was saying, 'Why do we all work like crazy all the hours of the day all the days of the week the grinding toil and run around like maniacs and get to the end of the long day exhausted and sleep badly and get up in the morning and do it all over again?' She looked at me with eyes too wide. 'Why?'

The next day – honestly, the very next day, I think it was – she came home from the plant and said, 'They called us in for a meeting and said would anyone like to work a four-day week? Is that incredible timing or what?'

'Synchronicity,' I agreed. 'A sign and wonder.'

'What do you think?' she asked. 'We've got more money than we ever spend, haven't we, we could afford for me to work a day less and take a deep breath and assess what the hell I'm doing with my life.'

'We're saving the money for when you get pregnant,' I reminded her.

'How much have we got so far?' Alli asked.

'Four thousand, three hundred and sixty-seven pounds,' I said.

'You see?' she said. 'Plenty.'

I was going down the stairs. Tosh was coming up. I'm calling him Tosh because he reminds me of Peter Tosh, the reggae musician. I don't know his real name, he hasn't been living here that long. He comes from Birmingham. Well, either that or he's putting on a Brummie accent for his own amusement. Which he may well be doing. I do such things, so I don't see why other people shouldn't. Like, for example, whenever our paths cross (which is not that often) I always say, 'All right, Tosh?' which he will think is me saying, 'All right, mate?' or 'All right, pal?' when in my own head I'm saying, 'All right, Peter Tosh lookalike?' You see what I mean? I'm amusing myself, at no one else's expense. Don't you do that?

Anyway, as we passed on the stairs, I said, 'All right, Tosh?'

And he said, 'Fockin lift's out of action again. Fockin council. I'll be lite for the fockin gym.'

Neither of us had stopped. By now we'd passed and were some steps apart. I turned and called up, 'Now the lift's not working, you don't *need* to go to the gym. You can have all the exercise you want right here.'

Tosh stopped too and turned and stared down at me.

'Think of the money you'll save,' I said.

'Are you tryin to be foonay?' Tosh asked.

'Yes,' I said.

Tosh took a step towards me. But perhaps he realised that every step he took down he'd have to retake up, or perhaps he saw that I was not trying to be provocative. So he just shook his head and resumed his ascent, as I resumed my descent.

Peter Tosh was one of the original Wailers, by the way, along with Bunny Wailer and Bob Marley. Our dad had a stack of reggae records, which we children all listened to with him, dancing lazily around the lounge, when he was at home, permitted to live with us, but his favourite record was '(White Man) In Hammersmith Palais' by The Clash, which he said was about him. Joe Strummer and Mick Jones had written that song about our dad! It was so cool.

At some point, or perhaps gradually, I came to realise that this was not true, but I never thought that Dad was lying, not really, more that he was speaking figuratively. There used, after all, to be a reggae place called the Caribbean Club in Oxpens, between the college and the Westgate shopping centre, and often, Dad told us, he really *was* the only white man there.

No, it wasn't Dad, obviously, it was Mum who had the drive in our family, who made us all work hard at school. 'If you don't do better than your parents did, I'll see myself as a complete failure,' she told us often, a powerful, guilt-laden motivating tactic that was sadly ineffective.

I never take the lift myself, even though it almost always *is* working. I always climb the stairs, ever since we saw that locum doctor a couple of years ago who told us to 'Keep trying! You never know!' I asked her if there was anything I should do about the low sperm motility. 'You don't smoke, you don't drink, you don't use anabolic steroids,' she said. 'And this is good, it's all good.' For a moment she looked at a loss, then her eyes seemed to alight on something on her computer screen, I assume it was our address, and she said, 'You live in one of the towers? Which floor?'

'The eighth,' Alli told her.

'Perfect!' said the doctor, and she told me to always use the stairs. I would lose weight and get fitter and that would help with the depression, too, which to be fair it has.

***

Anyhow, I carried on down the stairs (while Tosh climbed to his place on the eleventh floor, so he could get changed and go back down and out to the gym) and walked to the Blackbird to meet Benny. My brother had texted me, and said he'd bike over. He lives in a tower too, and there are only five in our little city, these three in the Leys (Windrush, Evenlode and ours), one on Wood Farm and the one over at Northway where Benny resides. (Six, I suppose, if you count Hockmore in Cowley, but it's more of a block than a tower, isn't it?) How's that for a coincidence, eh? Although, come to think of it, neither of our other brothers lives in a tower. Lucy, our sister, does, but hers is one of those expensive private ones, all light and reflection. It's up in Liverpool. The Dockside Development or some such. No, Benny and I are the only true failures in our family.

I don't drink. It interfered with the medication, back in the day, so I stopped and got out of the habit. Alli likes a glass of white wine and she also likes to smoke weed watching telly on a Friday night, and I might join her for a toke or two, but that's about it. So I bought myself an orange juice and a pint of Guinness ready for Benny, since of course he was late as always. He claims that some of his buddies live on nothing but stout and smoke and he's going that way himself but he still needs carbohydrate. Pasta, bread, spuds. Benny reckons that good beer's got everything you need, almost. I'm amazed that he doesn't fall off his bike more often, frankly, but the beer doesn't seem to affect him any more (apart from the slurred speech, obviously). I'm bewildered, too, that he's still so thin. Benny's wiry, leanly muscled, he always was. You'd have thought all that beer would make him puffy or soggy but it hasn't, except for his face.

Benny came in breathing hard and sweating. We sat down and, before he could tell me what it was he wanted, I asked Benny if he thought that the Queen still had someone to warm her toilet seat for her. I said I'd been wondering about it again – did he remember how we discussed it years ago?

Benny said he did not remember, and that I was a pillock. Perhaps the Queen had a humble toilet-seat warmer, perhaps she had not, once upon a time, like in a fairy tale, but this was 2016 and she certainly did not have one today. He said that to talk like that was disrespectful to Her Majesty, poor old dear.

I said that actually, bro, it was 2018 now, in case he hadn't noticed. It worried me that those lost weekends of his seemed to have become lost years. And I was surprised to see that he'd become a rabid monarchist in his middle age. I always thought he was a republican. When I was a teenager I'd hear my older brother say things like, 'Them Russkies had the right idea, we should do with our lot what they done with the Romanovs.'

Benny said, 'Obvioushly, their toilet sheats will be warmed up automatic now, you plonker.'

One of the nice things about seeing Benny is that we can use words from our childhood – like pillock and plonker – that you don't hear much elsewhere. I had to agree he was probably right about the automation. It's happening in all sorts of industries, after all. 'I suppose the next advance,' I said, 'will be they'll have robots to do it for them, and maybe those robots will be life-like and resemble the Royal Household flunkeys of our childhood, and so restore the regal privilege and trad-ition of old.'

I thought this was a pretty comical picture I'd painted, I don't know about you. Benny just scowled like he couldn't believe how stupid I was, spouting my usual nonsense, but just then one of his old pals, Dex, passed our table. He spotted Benny and they gave each other a kind of slurred alcoholic hug. Dex asked Benny what he was doing in our neck of the woods. Benny said he was visiting his brother here. Dex acknowledged me with a cursory nod. He dragged a chair over and sat down, saying, 'I can't stop.' Great, I thought, that's him here for the duration.

'How's Lucy?' Dex asked. He'd always fancied our pretty sister. Everyone knew it, it was a bit of a stand-ing joke, a running gag, the rough lad's unrequited love for our stuck-up sister. 'She weren't doin too bad, were she?' Dex came here from Manchester with his family a long time ago, he went to school with Benny, down the road at Peers, but if you met him and he opened his mouth you'd think he arrived yesterday.

Benny told Dex that Lucy was living in a plush apartment in a glass tower in Liverpool. Dex grimaced and said, 'What's a lovely bird like your sister go and do a stupid thing like that for? Fuckin Liverpool?' He shook his head. 'The only good thing to come out a Liverpool's the M sixty fuckin two.'

I couldn't help laughing but Dex said, 'It's not funny, lad, it's fuckin tragic.'

Benny said it was great to see Dex, but he had to talk to his brother here about something. Dex took the hint and stood up. He shook hands with Benny and said, 'Say hello to your sister from me.' Then he pointed a crooked finger at me and added, 'And that goes for you too, lad,' making it sound like some kind of threat.

I took a sip of orange juice. 'What is it, bro?' I asked Benny.

'I'm a geniush,' he said.

'We all know that,' I assured him. 'But what do you want here, now, today?'

'I've had me an idea,' he said.

'Oh no,' I replied.

'In the form of an offer.' Benny smiled. 'From me to you.'

I was perplexed. There was nothing Benny had that I could possibly want. This is not an exaggeration. He owned the clothes he stood up in (or, at this moment, sat down in). He wore them every day, until they fell apart, frayed by his sharp elbows and bony knees, and then he went to the Animal Sanctuary shop where he tried on dead men's clothes and haggled over the price with Alli or whoever else happened to be volunteering that day.

'What kind of offer?' I asked.

In his one-bed council flat in Northway, Benny owned a broken sofa, a stained mattress, a number of empty cans he called ashtrays, ill-assorted pans and cutlery in the kitchen, and a toothbrush. He'd quite likely bought that second-hand.

'What ish a man's mosht preshious posheshion?' Benny asked. He peered at me, grinning, and swaying slightly where he sat.

'His honour?' I ventured. 'His memories? I could say his woman, bro, only unlike in all those country songs you love, women aren't men's possessions, are they? Not even in Nashville any more, I shouldn't think.'

'His sheed.' Benny beamed at me. Or if not at me, exactly, at least in my general direction. 'You shee?' he said. 'I'll give you my shperm, brother. We're practically the same DNA. Our genes are practically *ident*ical.' I swear Benny's eyes almost sparkled behind the dull sheen. 'I would do that for you, brother. I'd come round when it's the right time for Alli, in her shycle and all that, we'd have a quickie, it would mean nothing.'

I stared at my brother, unable to think of anything to say.

'I know what you're going to shay, you bashtard,' Benny said. 'You're going to shay I can't get it up no more. But I can, brother, and I will for you, I promish.'

Alli volunteers at the Animal Sanctuary shop on a Friday. Even though there's a sign on the door that says WHEN SHOP IS CLOSED, PLEASE DO NOT

LEAVE CONTRIBUTIONS OUTSIDE, almost every morning there are bags there, and often foxes or rats have ripped the bags open with their claws and had a look inside and scattered the contents across the pavement. Alli says that sometimes it's not rats or foxes but human beings who go through the bags left outside the charity shop, taking what they want and leaving what they don't want tossed about.

Alli is often the one to sort through donations made by kind people – whether during the day or the night – and she tells me about them. When she started there, she was astounded. 'You won't believe it,' she said. I imagined she was going to tell me about beautiful or precious or valuable objects, but no. 'Lots of the clothes we get aren't washed,' Alli said.

'Really?'

'Yes. Dirty clothes. Even underwear!'

'People donate their dirty underwear to a charity shop?' I asked. Alli was quite right: I could *not* believe it. The charity also, she told me, receives food-encrusted kitchen utensils. They get broken toys. They get books whose pages are stuck together from rising damp.

'Do people use the charity shop like a dump?' I asked Alli. 'Because it's closer than the recycling centre at Redbridge?'

Alli nodded, pensive. 'People are strange,' she said.

All sorts of other, useful things are donated, including clothes in good condition, i.e. washed before being handed in. The Animal Sanctuary shop is the only charity shop on the Leys, which means not only that it's a place to buy clothes at a reasonable price, it's the *only* place to buy clothes. Templars Retail Park is a bit of a schlepp. A lot of the inhabitants of our tower buy their clothes in the Animal Sanctuary shop, and I'm impressed by the way people have their own look or style and even in a little charity shop find garments to suit them. Like the Tunisian woman, Mariem, who unearths bright-coloured dresses. Or Tarek, the Syrian, who's always dressed in a suit with a white shirt, no tie, top button done up. Always. Tarek told me that the torturers pretend to hang their political prisoners, they string them up and after a period of intense pain and terror let them down again – apparently they find this amusing – and it's why you'll never see Tarek wear a tie.

Then there's Mido – who's always smoking and in a hurry, since the day he arrived here. He's probably organising and campaigning frantically among his fellow émigrés, lobbying our politicians and raising money, driven by ideals and anger and an exile's guilt. Even now, or especially now, when things are worse than before the Arab Spring. Anyway, Mido wears a leather jacket over pullovers and grey trousers. The pullovers change colour but they always look the same, just right somehow, those of a committed revolutionary.

How do I know these people get their clothes from the Animal Sanctuary shop? Because either Alli's actually sold the items or she recognises them, and we'll be coming out of the tower or walking along Cuddesdon Way to the park or going into the library, and she'll squeeze my hand in a particular manner, I can't even identify how, exactly, but I know it when I feel it, and after we've passed whoever was approaching us she'll lean towards me and whisper in my ear, 'Blouse.' Or, 'Skirt.' Or, 'Oxford United baseball cap.' (That was Mariem the Tunisian woman's husband, by the way.)

The clothes that Alli notices for herself are handmade ones. Baby clothes. Knitted cardigans and booties and so forth, and she'll buy them (at the price the manager sets, in case you were wondering; there's no staff discount in the charity shop) and bring them home.

'The trouble is,' I said, 'that we're losing twice over. We're losing the money you're no longer earning on Fridays at the plant, and we're also losing the money you spend on Fridays at the shop. Earn less, spend more: it's a recipe for financial disaster.'

But Alli understands my sense of humour. She knew I wasn't really complaining. I was teasing. She continued with her sporadic purchases, and there's a cardboard box in the second bedroom of our two-bedroom flat, which for the moment is where I work. Last week I realised that someone must have donated a large unopened pack of disposable nappies to the charity shop, because there was one in a second cardboard box on top of the first box in a corner of the room.

Some days, when I've got no specific reason to go out, I walk up and down the stairs anyway. I descend to the ground floor then turn around and climb. I don't stop at our eighth floor but carry on up to the top, fifteenth floor.

Malcolm lives down on the third floor, and is (according to his claim) the only occupant of our tower who's been here ever since it was opened in 1960. We sometimes chat on the stairs. He told me that for a period, in the late 1970s and early 80s, you could get on to the roof. On warm summer evenings a group of them would go up with a stereo and play reggae and drink beer and smoke spliffs. But then someone fell or jumped or was pushed off – Malcolm says he can't remember – and the council secured the door. It's a shame. I should think Alli and I might like to go up there and hang out; to have friends in the tower to hang out with. It's not like there's any other socialising area.

Anyway, I reach the fifteenth floor and turn around and go back down to our flat on the eighth. I sometimes do that twice a day. It makes a break from the translating work I do, which is very slow. My German isn't great, to be honest, and because they're technical manuals I often have to look up words that I wouldn't know even if I was fluent. Last year I calculated that I earn less in an average week than Alli does on a good day, and she said, 'You know what? After my maternity leave I'll go back to work full-time and you can be a house husband.'

'What we call in the tower a flat husband,' I said.

'An apartment husband,' Alli said, chuckling.

'A condominium husband,' I said. 'A husband who didn't use a condom and is now a full-time father.'

Alli gave me a kiss and I understood that she'd said that, about me looking after our future child, or children, to make me feel better about earning so little.

As I was saying, I walk up and down the stairs, like the doctor advised. It's efficient exercise – once I've done a complete loop I'm huffing and puffing, I can tell you – but it's also nice to see a neighbour or two, to say hello, to wish them a good day.

I have another habit that I enact for my own amusement but also, I hope, one that the recipients might enjoy: once I know where someone's from, when we meet on the stairs I say hello to them in their own language. '*Marhaban*,' I say to Mariem and her husband. I address Tarek formally, '*As-salaam Alaikum*,' he's such a serious man. And to Mido I say, '*Keef halak?*' 'Good, good,' he says, hurrying along.

Occasionally, if I'm feeling frivolous – and if I think the other person might not take it the wrong way – I'll say hello in an entirely inappropriate language. '*Buongiorno!*' I'll say, but I do it dramatically, theatrically, so the other person knows (I hope) that I'm doing so on purpose, I'm being playful, and you'd be surprised how often they'll respond in kind – '*Ciao!*' – and we smile at each other as we pass.

People are strange, it's true, but when we're not unhappy, and with a little tickle, people like to be skittish, frisky, if you only let them. That goes for different sorts of people, I've noticed. Occupants of the other towers in the city refer to ours as 'The Transit'. Ask anyone. People come into our tower from all over, I think of it like a beacon calling people who need a home. A sanctuary. Like churches were once, before their doors were locked. And then when people have sorted themselves out, they move on. (Apart from Malcolm and his wife, who never have.) Alli and I have our eye on a place in Barton, near the pool and the primary school, ex-council. It belongs to a work colleague of Alli's called Daina; she's dividing it in two, she'll live upstairs and we'd rent the downstairs, with access to the garden, and that's the clincher, Alli says: French windows a toddler can toddle out of on to the grass. A paddling pool from Argos on a summer's day. Washing on the line.

I told Alli of Benny's offer. She was aghast. 'How can you even consider such a thing?' she said. 'For even a moment?'

'It's not *my* idea,' I said. 'I'm not recommending it. Heaven forbid. But Benny made the suggestion and I thought I should let you know. Shouldn't I?'

'What exactly is between your ears?' Alli asked. 'Sometimes I think there's nothing but air. And in the air, midges and, like, moths are fluttering, those are your thoughts and that's it and there's nothing else.'

Alli put her head in her hands. I wanted to step over and hug her, but I didn't. I figured that wouldn't help. Then she raised her head, and said, 'I'd have a brain-damaged baby born with a drinking problem.'

'An unquenchable thirst,' I agreed.

'All my milk would never be enough,' she said. 'Anyway, you idiot, if I was going to receive sperm from one of your brothers, it would hardly be that one, would it?'

Benny and I have got two other brothers, the middle ones. Steve went to America years ago and we lost touch. 'I suppose I could try to track him down,' I said. 'Connect with him on Facebook, and send a message. *Hi Steve. Long time no see. How are you? How would you like to come home and impregnate my wife?*'

I suspect Alli wanted to keep scowling, really, but she couldn't help a little smile. 'What about Mick?' she said. 'He's got four kids already, one more shouldn't faze him.'

'Five,' I said. 'You forget that Lisa produced another in the spring.'

Alli shook her head. 'I can't keep up.'

I must admit that when Mick and Lisa announced the birth of their latest child it occurred to me that they were not being quite as irresponsible as Alli considered them to be, but were at some subconscious level compensating for us and our infertility. I mean, if sensate *Homo sapiens* should seek to reproduce themselves, so that two people together have two children (enough to propagate the species but not so many as to infest the planet), Mick and Lisa have helpfully fulfilled our quota too – plus one for Benny. He's got just the one daughter, Siobhan, who he hardly ever sees since he's not allowed to be within five hundred metres of his ex-partner, Siobhan's mother's place. When he did go round there last year in a bit of an emotional state and barged into their flat, she ended up giving him a hammering, and Benny needed stitches. What he didn't appreciate, I told him, was that he was the first person to be handed an exclusion order for his own protection.

Siobhan is thirteen now. She's into gymnastics and make-up. She adores her dad, and Benny likewise, he'd do anything for that girl. He showers her with gifts whenever he's flush, which I don't believe is often, to be fair. Siobhan's going to be a lovely cousin. She could be our number-one babysitter – when we move to Barton we'll be that much closer.

Alli looked forward to Fridays in the Animal Sanctuary shop. At first she said it was so much more reward-ing than on the line in the plant, meeting new people, serving her community. She said there was one old chap who came in every week, donated one book and bought another. The books he donated were all ones he'd bought previously, but he always rubbed out the price on the inside front cover. He told Alli he thought of the shop as his private library.

But lately Alli's been growing disillusioned. Maybe working in a charity shop causes a strange slow-burn stress, you can only do it for a while before you burn out. Last week, for example, she came home and told me that someone had donated a toilet seat.

'Please tell me it was in the original wrapping,' I said.

'Sort of,' Alli said. 'It was in the original cardboard box of the toilet seat they'd bought to replace it.'

'Are you telling me—?'

'A used toilet seat!' Alli cried. 'With yellow stains!'
She shook her head. 'Sometimes I don't know what
to make of this life. I mean most of us want to make a
better world but we'll always be human beings, right,
so we'll fuck things up one way or another. But why?'
She was speeding up towards full throttle again. 'Why?
Is it because all of us harbour enough cruelty, pervers-
ity and selfishness to fuck everything up? Or because
enough of a minority of people are overwhelmingly
cruel and greedy and perverse and psychotic and they
fuck everything up for the rest of us? Not to mention
for other living creatures and the earth itself! And let's
not forget, while we're about it, future generations,
eh?' There were tears in Alli's eyes now. 'I don't know,
love,' she said. 'I just don't know.'

I could see that Alli was spiralling again. I asked if she
had any weed and to my relief she said that she'd seen
Kristina in Lidl after work the day before, and Kristina
had given her some. And by coincidence during the
week someone had donated a DVD of *Koyaanisqatsi*,
did I remember that film? 'We used to have a video of it
and the tape got twisted, then we had a DVD but we lent
it to Maz and Bobby, and they lent us *Game of Thrones*
Season Three, only we've never swapped them back.'

I said that of course I remembered it, it was ideal.
That evening we watched *Koyaanisqatsi* and Alli
smoked weed and calmed down.

***

It was Malcolm on the third floor who you could say made it happen, in a way, one week later. He went looking for a nice item of clothing for Imelda, his wife, and got chatting with Alli. Imelda must be the largest lady in the tower, if not the entire estate. Malcolm once confided in me that his wife had put on weight every year of their married life. Then he rubbed his hands together and said, 'Me, I loves a big fat woman.' Malcolm treats his wife like a queen (I wouldn't be surprised if he warms the toilet seat for her). He often drops in to the Animal Sanctuary shop seeking something for Imelda to wear, and the incredible thing is that quite often he finds it. Indeed, Alli and the other volunteers put such outsize attire by, for Malcolm's personal consideration.

Anyhow, Alli and Malcolm were chatting, and Malcolm told her about how his daughter is with a useless, feckless wastrel yet miraculously their children are all fine and healthy. 'God's beautiful creatures.' He told her that heavy alcohol consumption affects sperm count and sperm quality, and it can also affect virility, but if despite all these obstacles a heavy-drinking male's sperm reaches a woman's egg and succeeds in fertilising it, there will be no detrimental effect on the resulting foetus. There are millions of spermatozoa in a single ejaculation: only one needs to make its way to a woman's fallopian tubes and fertilise her egg. Just one. Alli explained this to me, and said she'd been turning it all over in her mind.

'The thing is,' Alli said, 'I think we should take up Benny's offer.'

I was flummoxed. 'Are you insane?' I asked.

'I think we should give it a try,' she said. 'Oh, and I forgot to tell you, Daina's got her builder in, it's time to give notice to the council on this place.'

'Wow,' I said. 'When do you think we should do what needs to be done with Benny?'

'That's the thing,' Alli said. 'Tonight.'

'Tonight?'

'Yes, love. This evening is the most propitious moment in my monthly cycle.'

With trembling fingers I texted my brother. He said he'd bicycle over at seven. My first thought was to urge him to wear a helmet, and put lights on the bike. I was suddenly worried for his safety.

Alli had a glass of wine and smoked some weed. She said she needed to be relaxed, which I understood. I wished Benny and I had similar bodies, so that she might be able to shut her eyes, and imagine it was me attempting to help her make a baby, not my wiry, deranged brother. I expect you're wondering by now why we didn't go down a medical route: have Benny shoot his sperm into a bottle and Alli have an egg removed, these to be conjoined in a test tube and the fertilised egg reintroduced to Alli's womb. In a word, IVF. And I can't really answer this because the truth is that, during the hours after she informed me of her decision, neither Alli nor I discussed it in any further detail. I suspect she figured sex was more honest than a clinical procedure, it was messy in a way that she believed life should be.

I offered to stay in the flat but Alli let me go. At ten to seven I left and walked down the stairs. I had no plans beyond a slow wander to the Cowley Centre. It would give me time to work out whether buying flowers to take back for Alli would be appropriate.

As I passed the third-floor landing, I saw Malcolm through the glass of the fire door and pushed it open to say hello. He was still wearing his postal worker's uniform, he must have just come off shift. '*Bonjour, Monsieur Malcolm!*' I hailed him.

'There's my man,' he said. 'Hey, know what? I gat a treat for you.'

'For me?'

'Wait there,' Malcolm said, winking. He disappeared inside his flat, leaving the door open. I could hear him talking – to Imelda, presumably. I could hear a clinking of glass. Imelda raised her voice, Malcolm sounded like he was pleading with and mollifying her. Then he came out, wearing his duffel coat and a woollen cap and carrying a plastic carrier bag of bottles.

'Come wid me, man,' Malcolm said. 'I gwan show you some ting.' He stepped over to the lift, and pushed the button. Like some kind of conjuring trick, the doors opened at once.

I know, I know. Malcolm was clearly the last person to use the lift, coming home from work a couple of minutes earlier, yet to me at that moment it was still kind of magical, inviting, the way those doors opened for us instantly.

Inside the lift Malcolm pushed the button for the fifteenth floor. He winked again, but didn't say anything. He clearly had a surprise for me and didn't want to spoil it, so I didn't say anything either. Malcolm just hummed to himself as we rose through the tower, and somewhere around the tenth floor I recognised the tune: 'Legalise It', by none other than Peter Tosh himself! It took me right back to childhood, dancing around the lounge to our dad's records. I suppose it was perfectly logical that Malcolm would be humming it – if our dad was still alive, he'd be about the same age – but this was the kind of beautiful coincidence that gives me a glimpse of patterns which lie in the depths of our existence, glimpses of an order in the universe, and our place in it, that we can only dream of, yet might actually, after all, be real.

The lift reached the fifteenth floor and the doors opened. Malcolm stepped on to the landing and took a key out of his pocket and held it up for me to see, giving it a tiny little shake. 'This for you, man,' he said. 'I bin wantin to do this ting ever since I done tell you about it. Me brother work in the Buildins and I ask him. He say no, but I tell him it only be a one-off, I promise, and he relent.'

Malcolm used the key to unlock a panel on the wall, gaining access to some kind of control box. He pushed some numbered buttons and suddenly there was a noise above our heads. I looked up: a retractable ladder stirred and unfolded, like some giant insect awakening, and reached down to the floor. Then a door, to which these stairs gave access, opened. We climbed the staircase and stepped through the door on to the roof. Malcolm strolled a few yards then put the carrier bag down and spread his arms wide and turned around, breathing deeply, as if the air up here was cleaner than down below. Perhaps it was.

'I've not bin up here for *years*, man,' he said.

I walked around the roof – not too close to the edge, even though there's a bit of a barrier, as I lack a head for heights – and looked down on the estate. Cars and occasional buses slid to and fro along Blackbird Leys Road. In amongst the traffic, illuminated intermittently by the headlights of the passing vehicles, I spotted a lean, darkly clothed figure riding a bicycle, pedalling furiously. Late as ever.

I returned to the middle of the roof. Malcolm had built himself a big spliff and flipped the tops off a couple of bottles. He passed a Red Stripe to me.

'Like the old days!' Malcolm said, chuckling.

We drank the Jamaican lager. It was cold and unfamiliar to me and tasted really good. It was one of those still autumn evenings, barely any breeze even up on the roof of the tower. I looked up and could see no stars above – whether because of clouds or urban light pollution I wasn't sure.

Malcolm passed me his spliff and I smoked some, and drank some more beer. I thanked him for bringing me up here. I said it meant a lot to me that he had done it.

'In dem days most times I come up with me crew,' Malcolm said. 'But some time I come up on me own, you know? And I look out over the city north and south, east and west, I see the buildins and the lights, I hear the noise like the sea churnin below, and you know what I say to meself? I say this your city, Malcolm Garner. It belong to you. As you look upon it, so do you occupy it. It all yours.' There was only me but he could have been addressing his old crew up there on the roof. Then he pointed at me. 'And it all yours, too, man. It all of ours, you see? We are the people. We below but we come from on high. We be the kings and the queens a dis mortal world, there is none above us but the Lord.' Malcolm raised his arms up and looked all around. 'How great are his signs!' he said. 'And how mighty are his wonders! His kingdom is an everlasting kingdom, and his dominion is from generation to generation!'

Malcolm stopped talking. He took a deep breath, and sighed. Then he turned in my direction and peered at me in the semi-darkness. 'What the matter, man?' he asked. 'Why you cryin for?'

I sniffed and said I was fine, I was just emotional, that was all. I had things going on in my life. And what he said had affected me. We drank some more cool beer in the still autumn evening, and looked out over the lights and the traffic in the churning urban ocean below. There are so many of us, that's what's so hard to get your head around. A multitude of floundering creatures, plunging, lunging, towards our misbegotten destinies.

Blood Moon

They swam in the warm blue sea, or lolled in the hotel pool. Jemma let the sun dry her skin then dragged her lounger into the shade of a parasol. Mark dozed in the open, flesh baking. In their apartment after lunch they made love, lazily. Mark fetched water from the fridge. He was at ease naked in the heat. He had the loose paunch of an ex-athlete and it did not bother him. Perhaps having made a living for over ten years at his sport permitted him this premature middle age. Only his comically white buttocks let him down.

'You deserve a naturist holiday,' Jemma told him.

He took this as a compliment. 'I think you're right, love.'

In the afternoon they walked up away from the village, along overgrown paths, holding hands until sweat in their palms slid them apart. When they passed through a layer of scented air, Jemma broke off leaves and rubbed them between her fingers. Thyme. She raised her hands to her lover and he smelled the herbs too, identified them or attempted to. Fennel. They plucked ripe wild figs off trees. Small fierce sweet blackberries.

Bony cows were chained singly in dusty fields. Occasional rank odour of goats. Chickens roamed, pecking at the hard ground like some odd species of archaeologist. They disturbed a hare, which sprang up and bounded off through an olive grove. Spiders laid webs across plants, woven with a tighter mesh than their English counterparts, fine as the material of white tights. Time and again in the warm air came the scent of oregano.

On their third day, grey clouds rolled over the mountains. Breezes stirred the canes. Warm rain fell soft and silent. The following morning the sky was clear blue again.

They swam and dozed, read, made love, rambled.

After they'd showered they sat on the balcony of their apartment. Mark in white T-shirt and green shorts; Jemma's white dress, brown muscular limbs. Mark downed a beer. Jemma drank fruit they'd found or bought and blended into cocktails that picked her up as the beer dulled him. Fig, blackberry, orange. Then they strolled down to the restaurants along the shore.

There were eight establishments. Waiters importuned potential customers as they passed by. Jemma and Mark studied the menus, ate in a different place each night. Their week-long holiday meant that all but one would get their custom.

'I find it hard to convey to you,' Jemma said, 'how much I love Mediterranean food.' Tzatziki: yoghurt with cucumbers, garlic and dill. Sardines baked in a dish with onion, red and yellow peppers. Subtle detonations of taste in her mouth. They swapped spoonfuls off each other's plate. 'You can hardly taste the nutmeg,' she said of his moussaka. 'It's just there.'

'This one has the best chef,' Mark agreed. 'Maybe we should come back here on our last night.'

They ordered a carafe of white wine. Jemma sipped a glassful. Mark worked his way through the rest.

'I'm going to run a 10K in the morning,' she told him.

He looked at her, and shook his head. 'You're insane, love.'

'Pre-season starts next week.'

'Exactly.'

Jemma laughed. 'You want me to emulate your first-day-of-training stories?'

'That was back in the old days. By the time I quit it'd got serious.' He took a gulp of wine. 'I don't miss it.'

'The throwing-up?'

'The seriousness. I don't have your dedication, love. I never did.'

'So you're saying a comeback's out of the question?'

Mark smiled. They drank the wine. The waiters were tardy bringing the bill. Mark reckoned they kept the tables as fully occupied as possible to attract further customers. The emptier the restaurant, and less busy the staff, the longer it took for the bill to arrive. But Jemma and Mark were in no hurry. They watched the full moon rise over the sea. Jemma reached across and took Mark's hand, and when he looked at her, she smiled. He nodded. He understood her, and she him.

'You know that phrase, Jem,' Mark said, '"the prime of life"? That's what I'm thinking. You're in the prime of life, love.'

He was a little drunk now, she thought; though she hoped it was not just the wine talking.

'You're fucking gorgeous, Jem,' Mark continued. 'I don't even mind men looking at you.'

'What men?' Jemma said.

'Every other man we pass. You turn people's heads.' He lifted Jemma's hand and raised it to his lips and kissed it. 'I don't blame them.'

They walked up away from the restaurants, the one or two bars. Night had fallen, but the air was so warm still. When they reached their hotel Mark stepped off the pavement to the trellised walkway, but felt himself tugged back. Jemma had paused.

'Do you want to walk a little longer?' she asked.

Mark yawned. 'I'm asleep on my feet, love.'

'I think I'll walk a little.'

'On your own? You sure?'

She nodded.

'Will you be all right?'

'Of course, Mark.'

'I can come with you.'

'Don't be silly. I won't be long.'

He let go of her hand. 'If you see that blood moon they're on about, I want a full description in the morning.'

'Leave the key in one of my beach shoes, yeh? Outside the door.'

'Sure.' Mark reached out and took her hand again and leaned towards her and kissed her. 'Don't get lost.'

Jemma kissed him and turned and walked on. She could hear the slap of his flip-flops recede along the covered walkway; caught glimpses of his white T-shirt, almost parallel to her, between the foliage. Other tourists, in front of and behind her, made their way towards their own villas or apartments, further inland. A young couple passed in the other direction.

The higher up of the two little supermarkets was still open. She turned right and walked past the big hotel and a small complex of apartments, then a couple of locals' houses, and on out of the light of street lamps and windows. The moon seemed to have disappeared, presumably behind clouds. In the darkness, sounds magnified, became uncanny. The digital repetition of cicadas. She caught the scent of jasmine.

The body came out of the blackness behind her. Before she could react, to turn or run, his hands were on her shoulders. Then he was pulling her. He had both his arms around her neck and was scurrying backwards. Jemma tried to stay on her feet, not to lose her footing and have him drag her, so she skipped in reverse, her hands on his arms, not trying to wrest them free from her neck but rather using them like a bar, lifting her weight a little to make it easier to back-pedal.

The man hauled her off the tarmac, over gravel and off it on to grass. He pulled her with his arms around her neck, she grasping his arms and hopping backwards, like some macabre parody of a ballroom dance. They were under trees in the darkness and the man slowed down. He fell backwards on to the grass, taking Jemma with him, and twisting to his left, or trying to, but she put her right foot towards the ground and then pushed off it to stop him putting her face down, him on top of her.

Jemma hit the earth on her left side with a thump. The man had only accomplished half his aim and now attempted to complete it. Jemma bent her knees and pushed both feet. She had lost one of her sandals, the left foot. She would not let him get her prostrate upon the ground. He used his whole body, pushing against her; she could feel his stomach, hips, knees, like separate weapons he deployed but he could not turn her over so long as she kept her feet where they were. If her feet were locked against the ground, then as he turned her body with the parts of his body, so her legs acted as a lever and he could only lift her, and himself be lifted in the air on the pivot of her bent muscular legs.

But he would not give up. He grunted as he persevered. She could not tell if he muttered words. She did not know whether he was Greek or foreigner. She was grunting too and sweating. She could smell him. A smell of meat. She tried to prise his arms from around her neck but she did not believe that she could do so. Still, she could lessen the pressure of his stranglehold squeezing her neck, weakening her resistance.

Then all of a sudden he gave up and relinquished his grip around her neck. She threw her head back at him, a battering ram, but made no contact. The man had relaxed too the press of his body against her. Still pushing hard against the ground with her legs, Jemma propelled herself backwards, and in that moment of unintentional momentum she was falling against him, only he wasn't there any more, he was heaving himself around her, from behind to her side, and then as she came to rest upon her back on the hard soil he was clambering on top of her.

A fiendish manoeuvre. But Jemma kept her knees bent, up in the air now, so that he could not reach his right leg over them and across her lower body. His upper body was on top of hers, though, weighting her down. She reached up and spread the fingers of her right hand across his face and pushed him up away from her. He grasped her wrist with his left hand but he could not break her grip on his face.

With his right hand the man did something to Jemma's left cheek. Had he slapped or punched her? With no swing and so little impact. It did not hurt but still, she grabbed his right wrist with her left hand and held it away from her head. He tried to free his hand, twisting and jerking it; she held his wrist in her grasp. Again, it was like a kind of choreography, a frantic *pas de deux* of their two conjoined limbs.

Still the man tried to clamber over Jemma, but he could not surmount her raised right leg. An idea burst in her head. It was not original. In fact it was a copy of what her assailant had done. But it was brilliant. She pushed against him with all her strength, so that he had to use his full weight and power to keep her where she was, then suddenly she stopped pushing and fell back and as she fell she rolled him all the way over her until he was on his back and it was she who lay on top of him. Her hand was no longer on his face.

Jemma gripped the man's right wrist with her left hand, he had her right wrist in his left hand. He spat a sound, a syllable, for sure, a one-syllable word, a curse, but she did not know it.

Jemma was on top of the man, she had the advantage, surely, but she could not see what to do with it. She wanted to raise herself up, away from him, but that would allow him release, so she lay on his chest, her face too close to his, and in the darkness she less saw than felt his head jerk up towards her and his forehead thump against hers.

Stunned, Jemma lost her grip on the man's wrist and, her body floppy, she was on her back again and this time he had his legs between hers. She heard another curse then understood it had issued from her own mouth. She had not noticed until now but in the struggle her short white dress had ridden up her thighs, was crimped around her groin and buttocks, conspiring to make things easier for him. His right hand was yanking her knickers loose. Trying to tear them off her.

He held her right arm against the ground with his left hand, but her left hand was free. She raised her hand to his head and felt around for something to grab – hair, beard – she found his right ear and gripped the lobe tight in her fingers and pulled his head towards her and sank her teeth into his right cheek.

The man yelled in pain. His right hand was on her left hand, trying to prise her fingers from his earlobe, but that would not help him, he could not get to her teeth. He pulled her fingers off his ear and now he held both her arms – her left hand and her right wrist – but she had a lump of his fleshy cheek clamped between her jaws. He was groaning, moaning in pain and rage, pinning her down yet trapped himself. If she opened her mouth she was done for. There was a taste on her tongue. It was him, her attacker, her rapist, she could begin to consume him. He lowed like a beast of burden.

She felt his grip on her arms loosen and then he brought both his hands bunched into fists against her head, one on either side at the same time, like cymbals clashing, like a skull-shaped, double-sided drum. The shock, the boom, made her mouth go slack and he pulled himself loose from her jaws. He raised his head and upper body out of range away from her but she went after him. She put both her arms around his neck and though he held himself up for a moment, and tried to prise her arms loose with his fingers, her weight pulled him down until she lay back on the dry grass and he lay upon her, in her close embrace. Now he could not easily punch her, nor pin her wrists.

Jemma tried to bite the man again but perhaps he foresaw this and took one hand off her arm and pressed his palm against her forehead, pinning her head to the ground, his vulnerable flesh just out of reach of her teeth.

Jemma could feel the man's chest on hers, rising and falling, his lungs heaving. His breath was hot and odorous. The stink of meat, and beer, and tobacco. He was breathing hard, so close to her, and she understood that though he was considerably heavier than her, and somewhat stronger, he was much less fit. She had more stamina. He was tiring. The longer it went on, the more he would weaken.

His other hand was no longer on her arms. She hugged him unopposed. Then she realised that he was once more tugging at her knickers. She felt their seams bite into the flesh of her waist, her thigh, then she heard the sound or sensed somehow the cotton fabric ripping. And then his fingers upon her, groping, finding her. She felt something else, metal, his belt buckle being undone, and she knew he was unzipping or unbuttoning his flies.

'No,' she said, and she heard it as a snarl, a protest, a promise. 'No, you fucker.'

Jemma raised her legs and wrapped them around the man's torso and locked them at the ankles and squeezed as hard as she could. It made no difference, the man continued fumbling where his groin met hers. She felt something in her vagina, was it a finger or fingers or his thing? She groaned with the effort to squeeze his sides, to bend his ribs until they snapped, to press the precious rotten air out of his lungs. It did not affect him.

But then it did.

The man's hand was gone from her crotch and was on her leg, and the other hand had left her forehead and was on her other leg, trying to lever her legs apart. They were locked at the ankles. He tugged at her knees but he was not strong enough to prise them loose.

Now her head was no longer pressed against the ground. She unwrapped her arms from around his neck and held his head between her hands in what might have been an affectionate gesture but was merely to measure in the darkness exactly where his face was. Flexing the muscles of her neck she thrust her face towards his, bowing her head as she did so, smashing into him.

The man yelled. His hands went slack on her legs. Just as she felt them at her wrists she butted him again, and again he cried out. He grasped her wrists and freed his head and raised it away from her, but he could only escape so far because her legs wrapped around his torso kept him there.

Jemma felt moisture on her face. For a moment she wondered whether it was raining but this was not wet like rain. It was blood dripping. His hands let go of her wrists and she saw them go to his face, both to protect himself from further assault and to trace the damage there.

Jemma unlocked her ankles and unwrapped her legs from around the man's torso and levered her knees between her body and his. She drew her knees up against her chest and walked her feet up over his stomach then got a purchase against him and, grabbing his collar, she pushed him up away into the air and rolled over to her right side. The man toppled on to his back. He felt his face and howled.

These things Jemma could see. There was more light than there had been, though there were many hours until dawn. The clouds must have cleared away again but the moon was the wrong colour; it cast not a silvery light but orange or red or rusty. She rolled back the other way and used the rolling motion to raise herself to her feet. She made out the man lying on his back and stepped towards him and jumped into the air. She wanted to burst all the oxygen out of his lungs, his gasping unfit smoker's lungs, and landed on his stomach. Maybe she had missed his lungs entirely but he moaned and his torso and legs scissored towards each other. As she stumbled off him he rolled on to his side curled up with one hand on his belly. Jemma stamped on the side of his waist then on his ribs, then his shoulder, then his head. With the heel of her right foot. She was right-footed, after all.

The man groaned. At first she thought that he was merely making a sound of suffering but then she understood that his lamentation consisted of words. Was he begging for mercy? Forgiveness? She did not know.

She wanted to shut him up. With her right foot she pushed him on to his back and knelt with one knee on his chest, the other with her shin across his neck. He tried to push her off but his efforts were feeble, and when he left his face uncovered she punched it until he returned his hand to its protection. As he weakened she shifted her weight from the knee upon his chest to her shin across his windpipe. When she was sure he was barely conscious she pressed a little longer then leaned back on to her feet and stood up.

The silence was profound save for her own exhausted gasping for breath. Then the incessant sound of cicadas re-entered her hearing. The blood moon was up above the olive grove. Jemma staggered away. She saw the rock and did not think but bent towards it, and pushed and pulled it loose and lifted it.

Holding the rock heavy before her, like some grossly pregnant woman, Jemma lurched back to where she'd been. The man still lay, moaning softly. She could see where his hand was, covering his face. She stood in contemplation, holding the rock, like one of those nuns who burden themselves the better to rid their minds of distraction.

Jemma stood, trembling. She thought that it was anger that had propelled her but it was not. It was aggression, a warrior instinct sprung forth from deep in her DNA. No, this was anger, now, coming after the fight, an energy flowing not through her muscles but through her blood, coursing through her veins and up into her brain. How dare he?

How dare he?

In their strength and conditioning tests at the end of last season she'd bench-pressed a hundred and ten pounds. Jemma bent her knees then pushed up from the ground to help her lift the weight in her hands. She raised the rock above her head.

Cinema

The mother took her children into the sweet shop. The boy chose a bag of pear drops and the girl chose a chocolate bar. Their mother paid and they left.

At the cinema the mother asked her friend, the usherette, if she would look after her son while she took the girl to the doctor.

'I'll keep an eye on him for you,' the friend said.

'Be a good boy,' the mother said. He watched her depart with his sister.

The usherette led the boy into the auditorium and sat him down in a seat at the back, at the end of the row, close to the door. 'Stay there,' she said, and disappeared.

The lights went down. *One Hundred and One Dalmatians* began. The boy sat spellbound. His mother had twisted the top of the paper bag of pear drops and the boy gripped the twist of paper, forgetting the sweets inside, so enthralled was he by the movie.

At the end of the film the lights came up. People rose from their seats and left. For a while the boy was alone in the auditorium. In time other people came in, in ones and twos, sitting here and there. They took off their coats and draped them over the seats or folded them over their knees. A large man sat in front of the boy. The boy remembered his pear drops and opened the bag and put one in his mouth. He thought of his mother and his sister in the waiting room of the doctor's surgery. Perhaps it was very busy today, with lots of sick people going in and out.

A woman sat beside the boy. The next film began. After the animation of Walt Disney, this was live action. A Western. It was not at first as alluring as *One Hundred and One Dalmatians* but the boy gave his attention to it, and was drawn in. He remembered his bag of sweets and sucked on another pear drop. The film continued. There were horses, and cattle.

The large man blocked the boy's view; he had to move his own head from side to side to see what was happening on the screen.

The cowboys in the film had arguments, the boy was not sure why. His grip on the twist of paper loosened and he dropped his bag of sweets. The bag broke and the sticky pear drops rolled across the dusty carpet.

The woman beside the boy leaned over and whispered to him, telling him it was all right, she had sweets too, he could have one of hers.

The boy took one of the woman's mints and tried to watch the film, but the big man sat in front of him, his wide shoulders and head blocking the screen.

The woman beside the boy leaned over and whispered to him, telling him he could sit on her lap to watch the film. She lifted him with seeming ease.

In the film two cowboys had a fight. As they struggled on the ground one of them kicked aside something covering a gaping hole. In the hole were snakes, many of them, all squirming around. The boy watched sitting on the woman's lap and the woman stroked his bare legs. The men wrestled each other, drawing closer to the snakepit.

The boy watched the men fighting, transfixed, as the snakes writhed in the pit. The woman stroked his calves, over his knees, his thighs. One of the cowboys fell into the snakepit. He screamed but it was no good. The other cowboy crawled to the edge of the pit and watched as his rival surely died in agony.

The cowboy rode out on to the open plain. The boy felt himself being lifted up and placed back in his seat. Then the woman rose and sidled off along the row of seats away from him and disappeared.

The film ended. The lights came up. The big man in front of the boy rose and left. The other spectators got up, carrying or pulling on their coats, and departed in ones and twos.

The boy thought that if his little sister had to go to the hospital again, his mother could surely leave her there awhile and come to collect him from the cinema. He watched as other people came in, but not his mother. In time, the lights went down, and another film began.

Through the Tunnel

The girl, her father, her older brother, Sol, and his friend, Bobby, walked from the house across a cornfield to the cliff. At the top there were two downward paths: a steep one to the left and an easier one to the right. Her father took the right-hand path.

'How do you know which one to follow?' Stella asked.

'Jif told me.'

They descended in single file, the boys at the back, speaking to each other in seemingly random words, or barely intelligible scraps of sentences, that prompted imbecilic laughter.

'We've travelled all this way,' Stella said, 'to where Mum and Jif came as children, and they can't even come to the beach.'

'We'll get them there before the end of the week,' her father assured her.

Halfway down the cliff path Stella saw a long sandy beach open out before her, populated by a multitude of semi-naked humans. Glancing to the left, she saw another bay with pockets of sand between rocks, uninhabited.

The boys threw off their shirts and ran, kicking water at each other, into the sea.

'Hang on,' the girl called, but they did not wait for her. Her father spread suncream over her shoulders and back. He applied it to his own large, white body and lay down on a towel to read a book, pages shaded by the brim of a straw hat. Stella swam in the warm, still sea, then wandered along the beach. Children built sandcastles, dogs ran, a family played a strange variation of rounders, pot-bellied men comically athletic. Some women were bare-breasted: all of their bosoms were different, Stella found it hard not to stare. Everyone was dark, their skin deeply tanned. A young girl caught her eye and threw a frisbee in her direction but she ignored it.

Her father dozed. She could not see the boys. They did not emerge from the ocean for hours. It was as if they'd visited Neptune's underwater kingdom.

'It's not healthy shit,' Stella's mother said. 'It's pestilential filth. The stink of it turns my stomach and it's mine.'

The girl sat cross-legged on the window ledge. Her father sat on the side of the bed.

'My body takes food and rather than extracting nutrients infects it with the poison and expels it with a kind of mischievous glee.'

'It,' Stella's father said. 'It.'

'Cancer, then.'

'I should be the one looking after you.'

'I won't let you. Jif knows my pills. Anyhow, she's happy caring for me.'

'She's doing so. I wouldn't say she's happy.'

'Oh, she is. I promise you.'

Stella's mother slept and dozed through the day. Jif stayed with her. In the evening she came alive for an hour or two with a fitful, febrile energy. She was like a light bulb flickering on and off, a power line buzzing, short-circuiting, buzzing again. It was like pain kept cutting the supply.

'Sing to me, Sol,' she begged her son.

The girl's father poured wine, and lemonade, passed round bowls of nuts and olives. Sol extracted his guitar from its case and tuned it with solemn precision, then played simple chords and sang dreary songs. His friend Bobby bent forward and nodded along with each song, face hidden behind his long hair. It looked more like he was agreeing with the sentiment of the lyrics than feeling the beat.

'What a voice,' Sol's mother said, made happy, though it appeared that even the slight muscular activity of the faintest smile caused her pain, and it manifested as more of a grimace. 'Don't waste your talent, darling boy,' she said. 'Your father wasted his, don't do the same.'

Stella saw her father shake his head.

'Providing for one's family,' Jif said, 'teaching young people, that's hardly a waste of talent, surely?'

'Oh, do shut up,' the girl's mother said. 'You know nothing about it.' She turned to Stella and said, 'Read to me.'

The girl turned to her father, who rose and fetched a book from the pile he'd brought with them. Aunt Jif rose too and went to the kitchen. Stella's father handed a book to her.

'Hopkins,' he said. 'Your mother loves Hopkins.' The girl scanned the contents page, and looked up at him. He said, 'Any of them.'

The girl read, her mother listening with her eyes closed, until Jif called them into the dining room for supper. They ate fried rings of squid, and shrimps, with fried potatoes and salad.

In the morning Stella brought her mother a peach she'd picked in the garden. It was red and yellow and perfectly ripe.

'You've caught the sun already, darling,' her mother said. 'Thank God you've not got your father's skin.'

When Jif came in, Stella moved away to the window. Her mother seemed then to lose sight of her, still there in the room.

'You're loving this, aren't you?' her mother told her sister.

'What?'

'Your entire life you've been jealous of me, and now I'm dying, long before you, and in pain, and you're ministering to my wretched end. You must be relishing every minute.'

The girl's mother sat in a chair beside the bed, while her aunt changed the sheets. Stella perched on the windowsill. Her aunt did not say anything for a time. Then she did. 'Why would I be jealous of you?'

'Oh, come on. My looks. My figure. Look at yourself. My boyfriends. My brains: you worked so much harder than me and still got worse results. I went to Cambridge and you went— Where did you go again?'

Jif said nothing. She took the pillows out of their cases and put new ones on. The girl's mother waited patiently, but in the end she tired of waiting and said, 'My work. My family. All of it. I've felt your envy, emanating from your pitiful existence. Your loveless-ness. I thought there must be a man out there for my sister. Someone. Somewhere. Apparently not.'

Stella realised suddenly that her aunt had tears in her eyes and the next moment she gathered up the soiled linen and ran from the room.

'They cut off my breast,' her mother called after, 'and I was still more of a woman than you.'

The girl followed and watched Jif drop the bedding in the hallway and run with ungainly stride away across the garden.

***

Stella and her father walked through the cornfield. The boys were not with them. Sol had said he would join them later.

'Why is Mummy so mean?' Stella asked.

Her father stopped. He took his straw hat off and wiped his forehead, replaced the hat and resumed walking. 'Derangement,' he said. 'Illness, pain, medication. Any of these can throw a person off balance, and make them furious, and they take their anger out on those around them.'

The girl said, 'Dying must send anyone mad.'

'Indeed,' her father said.

'Is it making *you* mad, Daddy?' she asked.

'It is,' he said quietly.

When they reached the cliff, the girl said she wanted to explore the other bay today. Her father stopped and turned. He looked down the steep incline to the rocky cove below, and he scrutinised his daughter. He gazed back down the slope, frowning. She could almost hear the slow-motion deliberation of his brain. Responsibility for her safety versus allowing her freedom.

'Of course,' he said. He swung the bag off his shoulder and extracted from it the tube of suncream and a bottle of water. 'Have fun,' he said. 'Be careful. I'll be in the same place as yesterday. Join me there or see you back at the house for lunch.'

The girl clambered down the path. The last stretch was across a stone shelf and she jumped from it on to sand. She unbuckled her sandals then she took off her shirt and shorts, and put them in the bag with her towel and the things her father had given her. The cove was larger than it appeared from above, with rocks and sand hidden by the curve of the hill. It was uninhabited. Hers alone. Stella trotted to the water and waded in past big rocks. The water was so clear that it was impossible to tell how deep it was: stones, seaweed, a crab seemed close enough to touch. The girl was a strong swimmer, a winner of races, like her mother before her, who'd taught her to swim with correct, precise strokes; to gulp air efficiently. It was hard to recall that woman now.

Stella swam out until, treading water, she could see the wide, populous beach on the other side of the headland. She thought she could pick out her father, a bulky, white-skinned man on a red towel.

Swimming back to her own beach, Stella looked up and saw to her dismay half a dozen figures making their way down the steep path. She breaststroked slowly towards the shore. The group jumped in turn off the stone ledge then disappeared behind a large rock, then reappeared. They paused momentarily when they saw her bag, and looked around. The tallest one peered out to sea and must have discerned Stella's bobbing head, for she pointed towards her, and the others turned in her direction too, and all gazed towards her. Then, seemingly at a word from one of them, they all kicked off their shoes and stripped to their trunks or bikinis and ran to the water. There were three girls and three boys, each one black-haired, dark-skinned. She estimated that all were older than her. A fat boy was overtaken by the others, who screened him from her view, splashing through the shallows, until they plunged forward, and revealed him once more, wading clumsily after them.

They swam towards her. Were they going to attack? Should she turn and swim out and round to the big beach and her father's protection? Would she outpace them? Stella stayed where she was, treading water, indecisive. Then she realised that they were altering direction, swimming around a colossal rock. One after the other they climbed on to it, the tall girl first, who strode up across the sloping rock to its highest point and peered over the far side. The others followed her, the fat boy joining them eventually. Then the tall girl dived off the rock, out of Stella's sight. One of the boys watched her and after a few moments dived in too. As the second boy dived, the tall girl appeared, swimming back around the rock. One of the other girls dived in, then the third girl followed, and finally the fat boy jumped. After a while the tall girl dived in again.

Stella swam in close to the rock and floated, watching. The group of divers yelled things to each other in the language she did not understand. A craving to join them filled her; a hunger.

The tall girl looked down at her watching them, and called out to her. Stella had no idea what she was saying, this glorious princely figure, this princess. Was she telling her to stop watching them, to go away? But then with an unmistakeable gesture, the girl beckoned to her. Stella swam in and climbed up on to the rock. The group spoke to her and when they saw she did not understand they each shrugged with a philosophical air.

Up close, her eyes green, the tall girl was even more beautiful than from a distance. So too was one of the boys. If she could just continue to gaze at them, Stella would never need anything ever again, not food or sleep or shelter, the sight of them would sustain her. Then the tall girl urged her forward, inviting her to dive into the blue-green water into which they had all plunged. Stella leaned forward. On this side, the rock curved back underneath itself. She stood at the edge, raised her arms above her head, put both palms together and executed as technically faultless a dive as she could muster. When she came back up to the surface they were all clapping her and whistling. She swam slowly back and clambered up on to the rock. So they continued to take turns diving, and swimming around and climbing out of the sea. At one point the tall girl sat on the sloping rock and the others sat too all around her. They gazed out to sea or lay back and shielded their eyes. Stella joined them. In the hot sun her skin dried in minutes. She closed her eyes.

When Stella woke, she was alone. The girl looked to the beach and saw that her companions' stuff was gone. Had she dreamed them? Was she insane? Perhaps her brain was turning against her like her mother's. But when she reached the sand, she saw their footprints.

***

Stella searched for her brother and his friend. She tracked them down in long grass at the end of the garden. She heard them before she saw them and crept closer.

'I want it,' her brother said. 'I want you.'

'I don't want it,' his friend told him.

'Yes, you do. You just don't know you do.'

'I'm not ready,' Bobby said.

'I can feel you're ready,' Sol said. 'You know you are.'

They stopped talking and the girl could hear sounds as if they were eating, and murmurs and groans. She wanted to ease herself closer so that she could see. Equally, she did not want to. The boys stopped kissing and started speaking again.

'I don't know what I am,' her brother's friend said.

'I know what you are,' Sol told him. 'I can feel what you are. The body doesn't lie.'

'You're lucky,' Bobby said. 'It's simple for you.'

'Yes, I've always known what I am. But whatever you become eventually, now is now. Come on.'

'No,' Bobby said. 'No is no.'

'No, it's not. You're aching for it, you know you are. It'll be over in a second and you'll be free.'

Stella had heard enough. She wanted to hear more. She wanted to leave. She wanted to stay longer. She pushed herself backwards and slipped down into the ditch and crept away.

***

On the day following, after Jif had helped her sister wash, and changed the bedding, the girl said she had to leave but her mother asked what the hurry was and begged Stella to lie beside her.

'I want to hug you but it hurts so,' she said. 'Lie with me, darling.'

When she was on her own, Stella's mind amused itself, but it seemed unable to lying next to another person. Time barely passed. She stared at the ceiling.

'Believe it or not,' her mother said, 'I was like you at your age. Quiet. Watchful. Timid. It all changed quite suddenly, I don't even know when or how, exactly. I think something must have happened but I can't remember what it was. I realised everything was easier than I'd thought.'

Her mother did not move yet Stella sensed her attention shifting towards her.

'What do you love to do?' she asked.

The girl could not reply. There was nothing or there were too many things, she was unsure which.

'Tell me just one,' her mother persisted.

Stella thought as hard as she could but nothing came. She asked her mother why she had refused further treatment.

'What has your father told you?' her mother said. 'I've been through it once, it was horrible, the cancer returned. That's what they said. "We're sorry to have to tell you that it's returned." It never left. It was there all the time, lurking, a monster in a cave. I'm not going through that again.'

'What about us?' Stella asked. She turned to look at her mother, whose eyes were closed. The door opened and her aunt came in.

'Sorry,' Jif said. 'Got caught up with the farmer.' She carried a small white bowl, which she put on the bedside table before going to the window and drawing the curtain. 'I think your papa's getting ready for the beach.'

The girl rose from the bed. At the door she turned and watched her aunt take two slices of cucumber from the bowl and place them like coins over her mother's eyelids, where she lay so still.

Stella scampered down the steep path towards the cove. There would be no one there today, hers alone, a prospect that thrilled her yesterday and today filled her with sorrow. But when she skipped over the stone ledge and jumped down to the sand she saw them, all six, already there. They were out on the same rock as before. She swam out and joined them.

This time, when the tall girl and the others rested, Stella did not close her eyes. After a while they swam inshore. As they walked up the beach the handsome boy abruptly jumped on the other one and pulled him over. They wrestled on the wet sand. The victim was more muscular than his assailant. He turned the handsome boy, and pinned him down. The tall girl stood above them and called out what Stella guessed were numbers, one to ten, whereupon the boy let go his grip, and the two of them rolled over and climbed to their feet, laughing.

The tall girl, the princess, spoke to Stella. She guessed from the tone, and facial expression, that what was being uttered was a question, but had little idea of what it might be. Something related to what had just happened? The tall girl pointed to the fat boy and asked the same or a similar question. The fat boy shook his head and turned and began to walk away but the tall girl fetched him back and brought him before Stella and asked the question again, this time acting out the meaning so that Stella understood.

An advantage of having an older brother, of her particular brother anyhow, had been years of unwilling apprenticeship in trying to fight him off.

The fat boy was slow and clumsy. Stella tripped him easily and so long as she kept his bulk off her, was able to control his movement until she felt him tire. Sand on their skin was an abrasive. Stella pinned him down. She heard the tall girl count to ten, then relaxed her grip and climbed to her feet. The others applauded. The fat boy struggled to stand. The tall girl pointed to Stella's skin, and brushed off sand. Then she took her hand and led her back into the ocean to wash it off.

***

That evening they ate fish that had so many bones that by the time they'd unpicked them the fish was cold, its texture unpleasing. After their mother had gone to bed, Sol and his friend listened to music, sharing a pair of headphones, pressing their heads together and stretching the headphones over their two skulls. The girl's father and aunt played Scrabble. Stella watched. Jif said, 'You can play too if you like,' but she declined.

The two adults concentrated hard on their letters, with occasional glances at the board, and placed the tiles into words. The girl thought that there must be many things they would like to say – about the woman who was wife and sister to them, their respective loyalties, fears, resentments – and perhaps, she fancied, this game was in fact a search for words to express in code what they could not share in normal speech.

'My God has smote me,' the girl's mother said. 'Struck me down. Forsaken me.' It was morning. Stella had delivered a ripe fig, then sat on the deep windowsill. Her father had come in shortly after.

'He's smitten,' he said.

'What?'

'He wants you with Him.'

'You think this is funny? You're making fun of me? My illness an excuse for a pun.'

'Cancer is what, your God now? Is that where we are?'

The girl's mother closed her eyes and smiled, faintly. The pallor of her skin was different today. It was thinner than ever, thin like the page of a Bible. 'Perhaps She is.'

'The worse your God treats you, the deeper your faith in Him. Her. Whatever,' the girl's father mused. He sat on the edge of the bed holding his wife's bony hand.

'It's a punishment,' she said.

'What on earth for? What are you doing wrong? Raising a loving family? Doing good work? What kind of merciful God would punish that?'

'Have you forgotten the Old Testament?' The girl's mother still spoke with her eyes closed. Opening her eyelids was too uncomfortable. 'The one we ignored. The wrathful God. I failed to praise Her. Obey Her.'

The girl's father stroked his wife's hand.

'I cannot wait to shed this rotten body. To move through that tunnel towards the light. After that, who knows?'

'Indeed.'

The girl's mother did not open her eyes, but raising her weak voice she said, 'Come over here.'

Stella uncrossed her legs and slid off the sill and moved around the bed to stand beside her father. Her mother opened her eyes and saw the girl and said, 'You know your father is a heathen, Stella. Don't judge him too harshly. He thinks I might be recycled as carbon atoms, if I'm lucky. You take what he says with a pinch of salt and make up your own mind.'

The effort of speech was plain to see. Her mother closed her eyes. 'Look after each other,' she said.

'What about Sol?' Stella asked.

'He'll look after himself. Sol's sweet selfishness. He'll be all right.'

The girl watched the group file down the steep path towards her. There were only five of them today. Stella saw that the fat boy was not among them, and felt responsibility, guilt, triumph. When they came wading into the sea she saw that they each carried something with them. They greeted her. The tall girl raised her goggles to her head, and put the snorkel in her mouth, distorting her lips like a gumshield, as if about to enter combat underwater. Then she dived, and the others followed likewise. The girl swam after them, tracking their snorkels, but though the water was clear it rippled in the sun and the salt irritated her eyes and all she could really see was their blurred limbs swimming away from her. She climbed out on to the diving rock. Each time one of them came up to the surface, to let water out of their goggles or snorkel, they were a little further away, working along the rocks, until they'd all disappeared.

Stella dived from the rock and climbed back out and dived again, but it was no fun alone, so she sat back down and waited. Then a head bobbed up in front of her. The handsome boy climbed out. He removed his goggles and handed them to Stella, explaining how they worked. His instructions were incomprehensible but it didn't matter, she knew how to snorkel. She nodded gratefully. In the water she strapped them on and put the snorkel in her mouth. It tasted of salt and rubber. Stella dipped underwater and in so doing crossed from one realm of existence into a wholly different one, that felt like it had more dimensions. Fish of many colours darted here and there. A crab scuttled beneath a rock. Shrimps bobbed in their element. She saw this under-world vision with magical clarity and floated in it, enthralled.

Time altered in this new dimension, but whether it contracted or expanded Stella could not tell. She turned around reluctantly and snorkelled back the way she'd come. When she reached the rock and lifted her head and removed the goggles, she saw to her surprise that the boy was still alone. He jumped in and floated beside her. Stella gave him the goggles but he reached out and placed them on the rock and came back to her. She felt his arms under the water encircle her waist and draw her to him, then he was kissing her. His tongue was like a tentacle of an octopus in her mouth. He took hold of her hand and placed it on some hard object. It took her a moment to realise what it was. Before she could take her hand away he had wrapped his own hand tightly around hers and was jerking it up and down his penis. She pulled her mouth away from his and opened her eyes. The handsome boy's eyes were closed, then he opened them and stared at her with a look of ferocity. He moaned, then threw his fine head back, gasping. He let go of her and floated free. She looked down and saw a thin pale trail of what she understood was semen rise through the water, and turned and swam to the shore.

Soon the others came out, the handsome boy with them. There were only four. One of the girls was missing. Had she left and gone home earlier? Was she still snorkelling, oblivious to the passing of time? Had she drowned? Stella had no idea. She watched them go, waiting until they had reached the top of the cliff and disappeared before she followed.

At supper that evening they ate a small fish, whitebait or sardine or something; they must have consumed a hundred between them, it was carnage at the dinner table. The girl's mother and aunt reminisced.

'Do you remember, Jiffie, the owners of this house warning us to keep away from that unsafe wreck?'

'And the next day Mummy swam out to it.'

'She climbed on to it and waved.'

'Daddy was furious.'

'Did they have one of their arguments?'

'I'm sure they did.'

'They must have.'

***

Stella's mother's energy crackled and fizzed and then was gone. Her husband and sister helped her to bed. Sol did the washing-up. Stella dried. Bobby cleared the table, put things away.

'Doesn't it turn your stomach,' Sol said, 'Ma and Jif talking about Granny and Grandpa, calling them Mummy and Daddy?'

Stella laughed. 'Turn my stomach?'

'It's weird, though, isn't it? When we're that age, if I say, "Do you remember Mummy did this, Daddy did that," you can take me out and shoot me like a dog.'

Stella did not know what to say. She had not considered the possibility of remaining in touch with her unpleasant brother throughout her life. A dismal prospect. He surely enjoyed her company no more than she did his.

'Because *I'll* shoot *you*, Stell, I can tell you that for free.'

'What with?' Stella asked.

'His pistol,' Bobby said.

Sol grinned. 'A small silver derringer,' he said.

The drying-up cloth Stella was using was soaked through. She draped it over a chair and grabbed another.

'What do you do all day on the beach with Dad?' Sol asked.

'I go to a different beach, actually.'

'Friendly,' Sol said. 'Poor Dad. Not that I blame you.'

'What about you two?'

'We have a project, don't we, Bobby?'

Sol's friend smirked. Stella finished drying the last pan and put it on the table. She hung the towel over a chair and went to her room.

The next day the girl waited on the beach all morning. They did not come until midday. This time there were only three of them. Neither the fat boy nor the handsome boy were there. Nor was the girl who had not left with the others the day before. Her fate remained a mystery.

The tall girl stripped to her black bikini and took Stella's hand and led her into the sea. The muscular boy and the smaller girl followed. They swam out and around the rocks, in the opposite direction from the populous bay, further than they had been before. The tall girl climbed out on to a rock. It rose from the water in a gentle slope to a commanding height. The tall girl walked up it. Stella followed. At the top, she peered over the edge and looked down into a well of clear blue water. She could see stones on the sandy floor, how far away – how deep or shallow the chamber was – she had little idea.

The tall girl turned to the other two and spoke to them, and they each stepped to the side of the rock and dived into the well of water. The tall girl said something. Stella turned to her and the girl put a hand behind Stella's head and grasped her hair. She looked into Stella's eyes then pulled her towards her and kissed her on the mouth, briefly. Then she let go and said something else, took a deep breath, and dived.

Stella watched the tall girl's beautiful brown limbs plunge into the water, in a bubbling commotion. There was no sign of the other two. The water settled, and now Stella could see no trace of the tall girl either. She put her hands above her head, palms together, and dived. Even as she plummeted through the air, Stella understood what a terrible mistake she had made.

Once in the water all she could do was confirm that the other swimmers had magically, or infernally, departed. The girl swam around the grey inner walls of the chamber, looking for protrusions or pockets that might serve as a hand- or foothold. There were none. The grey rock was smooth. She could not climb out.

They had to have escaped underwater. Stella took a gulp of air and dived down. Here the rock was darker and dotted with clumps of seaweed, with limpets and shells. She rose to the surface and took in more air, resumed her search. The depth of water, she surmised, was about twice her height. Stella tried to scan the chamber methodically, noting a particular anemone here, a barnacle there, but there were so many.

Stella searched and returned to the surface, treading water, breathing hard, looking up at the sky, circular above the grey walls of her prison. This was a place made to die in. So this would be her time. How odd, she thought, to have come here for her mother's farewell holiday, and die before her. Then something stirred in her, an anger. A fury. She decided – some element within her decided – that she was damned if she was going to die today. No. She would not.

The girl swam down again, and again. Finally she found the hole, by lucky touch, her foot seemingly entering solid wall encrusted with seaweed, just above the sandy ocean floor. She peered into darkness, and reached in. There was space enough to enter, but why was there no light? Perhaps this was merely a niche and the tunnel out of the chamber remained to be discovered.

Stella rose to the surface, as vertically as she could, and put her hands against the wall to keep her position while getting her breath back. With a lungful of air, she dropped and found the outlet or cavity. Pushing hands and arms ahead of her, Stella eased herself into the opening. Her back touched and scraped against the ceiling, and she imagined the weight of rock above her. It might collapse at this moment and crush her at once and forever, fossilise her bones, mash her into the stone. She was now in utter darkness. Fronds of seaweed slithered through her fingers, or perhaps they were fish. How much longer could she hold her breath?

It was not light, exactly, but Stella realised she could make out vague shapes. Then the tunnel turned to the left and ahead of her was a rough circle, a green watery glimmer. Stella pushed through to it, her lungs burning, and kicked up to the surface, which she broke and opened her mouth and felt all the parts of her body to be mere accessories to lungs that heaved like bellows in the cavern of her torso, as she gulped precious air.

***

At the top of the cliff Stella met her father climbing up from his beach. He smiled from beneath his straw hat. They walked through the waist-high corn.

'Joining us for lunch today,' he said. 'You must be hungry. Been having fun?'

'I've been swimming,' the girl said. She had only put her shorts on over her bikini, wrapping the arms of her shirt around her waist.

'Make the most of it,' her father said. 'Last day tomorrow.'

'I've had enough of that bay,' Stella told him.

Jif asked Stella to fetch her mother for the cocktail hour. The girl walked barefoot on the flagstones. She heard her mother speaking, and stood outside the open door.

'I don't want them to remember me like this.'

'Don't be silly,' her father said.

'A skeleton. A monster.'

'They won't.'

'They will.'

'Darling.'

The girl advanced silently into the doorway. Her father sat on the far side of the bed. He said, 'Come here,' and bent forward. Her mother leaned towards him and let him embrace her bony frame in his fleshy bear-hug.

Stella stepped back out of the room, and knocked on the door.

***

They gathered on the terrace. The girl's father poured drinks. The girl's mother said that she was hungry, wasn't that a thing? She looked at Stella, her sunken eyes peering at her daughter. 'You look like you've been here for months, my brown-skinned girl,' she said. 'You could pass for a local.'

Sol and Bobby came out. His father asked Sol what they'd like to drink. Sol said they'd love a beer, they deserved one for sure. But first would everyone come and see?

The girl's father and Jif both moved towards her mother but she said, 'Stella, would you help me, darling?'

Stella let her mother clutch her arm as they followed Sol around the corner of the house. Her mother was so light. It was as if what was left of her was dry and insubstantial. Her bones were hollow, her skin was transparent, her organs were like dried sponges.

The huge double doors of the barn were open. Bobby stood behind an inflatable float lying on the ground. Bits of rope poked out from beneath it. Sol said, 'Stell, I need you to be Mum's stand-in.'

'Lie-in,' said Bobby, grinning. He fetched a dusty chair from a corner of the barn.

Sol had his sister lie down on the blow-up lounger. 'Pa, will you come this side? Jif, go on the other side.' Bobby returned to the head of the lilo. Sol was at the other end, by Stella's feet. 'Now, everyone pick up a handle.'

It became apparent that this referred to loops of rope. The four of them grasped one each.

'Lift on the count of three,' Sol said. 'One. Two. Three.'

The handles were part of a cradle of rope that fit snugly around the lilo. Stella was lifted in the air. Sol led the way as they carried her around the barn, parading her for their mother's benefit.

'We made it for you, Ma,' Sol said. 'I found all the rope in here. We're going to carry Ma down to the beach tomorrow,' he told the others.

Stella felt disappointed when they set her down. Her mother said, 'Oh, Sol, darling, you're so clever.' Her father lifted the lilo to admire the boys' knotwork. Bobby told him that the rope stretcher referenced fishing nets. Jif said that was very clever, considering they were by the sea.

'So thoughtful, darling,' Sol's mother told him.

In the morning Jif told everyone at breakfast that her sister had had a bad night. They postponed the expedition until the evening. The hours dragged. In the afternoon they packed most of their things, ready for an early taxi to the airport the following morning.

In the early evening they crossed the cornfield. Stella was weighed down with a backpack and a bag containing her mother's requirements and two bottles of champagne, glasses, candles. She undoubtedly bore the heaviest load. Sol, at his mother's feet, had a speaker tied over his shoulders, playing music he'd chosen. Or curated, as Bobby put it.

They picked their way carefully down the path, to the accompaniment of 'Marche pour la cérémonie des Turcs' by Jean-Baptiste Lully. Stella thought that maybe her brother was some kind of genius, because the music, in all its pompous beauty, made it seem as if their mother was a dying queen, being conveyed in regal splendour.

'Slowly,' said the girl's father. Her mother grimaced with every shift and lurch.

As they approached the beach they could see that, though it was a warm evening, the heat of the day was gone and there were few people left. The rest gathered their possessions and fled the English arriving in their strange royal procession; they trudged away towards the road at the far end of the beach, where the metal-work of the remaining cars glinted in the low sun.

The girl's father said, 'How about here?' Stella watched them lower her mother carefully to the sand. She put the bags down. Her mother had her eyes closed and lips tight shut. She opened them, and relaxed. 'Help me up, someone,' she said.

The girl's father and brother each held one of her mother's arms and walked her down to the sea. Jif knelt and removed her sister's sandals and they walked her into the shallows. They were all gathered around her.

'I loved the sea,' she said. 'Didn't I, Jiffie?'

'I've never seen it so calm,' Jif said.

Stella thought her aunt was right. The tide did not seem to be either coming in or going out. There were not even ripples breaking on the shore.

'"He made the storm be still,"' her father said, '"and the waves of the sea were hushed."'

'Would you like us to carry you into the sea, Mum?' Sol asked.

They walked back up the beach and helped the girl's mother on to the blow-up mattress, and lifted her once again and walked down to the water. Stella watched them. Apart from footwear, no one had removed any of their clothing. She had her bikini on under her T-shirt and shorts, so she shucked them off and followed the others, who were now in up to their knees and had rested the lilo on the calm ocean. It lifted gently in the almost imperceptible swell. The rope cradle fell loosely away. Sol pulled it from underneath and passed it to Bobby, who carried it out of the sea, the rope sodden and heavy, soaking his clothes.

Stella waded to the head of the lilo, where Bobby had been, and pushed it further out. Her father and Jif stayed with it for a stride or two, as the water came up their thighs, then let go. Stella carried on into the deepening water. It came up to her waist, her breast, then she kicked up and pushed her mother, afloat herself. 'How far do you want to go, Mummy?' she asked.

'Is that you?' her mother asked.

'Yes.'

'Let's swim out to the wreck. That'll show them.'

The girl floated slowly, lazily. She swam on her side and looked back. Sol was on the beach with Bobby, lighting candles which they stuck in the sand. Her father stood motionless, his big torso and head a silhouette against the setting sun, a statue in the water. Her aunt was on her knees in the shallows, her head in her hands.

Stella turned back and pushed the lilo away from the shore. The girl was a strong swimmer. She came from a long line of strong swimmers. She pushed her mother further out on the open sea.

Author's Note

Short stories are written between the long bouts of labour involved in writing novels and are more sharply focused snapshots of the times one has lived through.

'How to Tell a Short Story' (2019) was written for my friend Jane Pugh, storyteller, performer, teacher.

'Blue' (1995) is an out-take from my first novel, *In the Place of Fallen Leaves*, set in the small Devon village in which I grew up. Having finished the novel, I was still caught up in the lives of various characters and wrote a number of further stories about them, of which I kept this one.

In 2003 I was perplexed – along with millions of others by my government's rush to war, by our Prime Minister's tireless jet-setting efforts to rally a coalition for the invasion of Iraq, justified by 'intelligence' that any reader of the broadsheet press could see was questionable. My wife and I attended demonstrations with our small children on our shoulders. For six angry months writing seemed futile. My wife had a friend married to an army officer sent to Iraq. Thinking about them, 'Harvest' (2003) emerged.

'Fidelity' (2005) came out of tutoring on creative writing courses, and fretting about the role of the imagination in creative endeavour, and life in general.

I wrote a good deal about rave culture. 'Invisible Children' (2008) came later, after a doomed attempt to recapture that magical moment.

'Chemistry' (2008) is about families and migration. I married a half-Polish woman, and was greatly admiring of her Polish father. He had come to the UK at the end of the Second World War, and with the wave of EU immigration after 2004 he became an unofficial employment agent, putting young migrants in touch with Oxford residents who needed their cars fixing, walls plastering, houses cleaning. I was fascinated by the way in which, whatever anyone's views pro- or anti-immigration, individuals get on with life: making friends, love, money; making a new world.

The episode recounted in 'Hunters in the Forest' (2009) is entirely made-up, yet this story is probably the most autobiographical piece of fiction I've written.

I do not have a brother, but rather two sisters and one half-sister (plus three stepsisters and a lovely stepbrother), yet conflicts between brothers recur in my novels and stories, I can't explain it. 'Brothers at the Beach' (2011) is one such. I guess it's one of the variations of relationships within families, and a relief from the more usual dance between men and women, and between parents and children.

'Rapture' (2015) is a simple story about the strange combination of tedium and joy experienced in the early years of parenthood.

I wrote 'Generation to Generation' (2018) at a time when loved ones were ill or dying, while others were trying to make a child, and I wrote it for them, really.

Watching the Me Too movement explode was chastening for a man. Having lived through the radical feminism of the 1970s – women ran self-defence classes, reclaimed the night – I guess I had assumed that while there were still men out there capable of violent rape, young women no longer suffered routine sexual assault. How wrong I was. Our daughter was sixteen, and a keen sportswoman, who trained, on field or in gym, pretty much every day. Watching her and her team play football was to watch twenty-two powerful young women. In a way 'Blood Moon' (2018) was my homage to them.

'Cinema' (2018) was a memory that twisted into a brief narrative.

Martin Amis once said that half of our urge to write comes from our encounter with the world, the other half from our encounter with literature. I read 'Through the Tunnel' (2019, my version) by Doris Lessing, and images and snatches of conversation started falling into my mind. Where from? From lived experience, from imagination, from misremembered moments.

I can see the clear debt certain stories owe to particular writers, and to these (John Cheever, James Salter, Helen Simpson, Lucia Berlin, Doris Lessing) and countless others, I offer humble thanks.

From 2017–19 I was employed by the Royal Literary Fund to run a Reading Round group in Littlemore,

Oxford. This entailed selecting two or more pieces of work (customarily a story and a poem, with occasional non-fiction) to read aloud to the group. They had a photocopy to follow as I read aloud, or they could close their eyes and listen, as they wished.

I would like to thank the RLF for my inclusion in this enlightened scheme, in particular Steve Cook, Katharine McMahon, Martina Evans and Marina Benjamin.

And warmest regards too to Mel Horwood, Jennet Batten, Pippa Gwilliam, Peter Agulnik, Maggie Campbell, Alice Daglish, Bridget Jennings, Rita Bevan, Marina Heeley, Lizzie Jamison, Anna Thomas and Brigit de Waal, core members of the group with whom this rewarding experience was shared.

Many thanks to Victoria Hobbs and all at AM Heath; and all at Bloomsbury, especially Alexandra Pringle, Allegra LeFanu, Lauren Whybrow and Sarah-Jane Forder.

And to Hania, my love, may the long story continue.

A NOTE ON THE TYPE

The text of this book is set in Fournier. Fournier is derived from the *romain du roi*, which was created towards the end of the seventeenth century from designs made by a committee of the Académie of Sciences for the exclusive use of the Imprimerie Royale. The original Fournier types were cut by the famous Paris founder Pierre Simon Fournier in about 1742. These types were some of the most influential designs of the eight and are counted among the earliest examples of the 'transitional' style of typeface. This Monotype version dates from 1924. Fournier is a light, clear face whose distinctive features are capital letters that are quite tall and bold in relation to the lower-case letters, and *decorative italics, which show the influence of the calligraphy of Fournier's time*.

TIM
PEARS
THE WEST COUNTRY TRILOGY

'Unsurpassed'
The Times

'Mesmerising'
Country Life

'Luminous'
Observer

'Lush, languorous, melodic prose'
BBC *Countryfile*

'Brilliantly captured voices'
Daily Mail

'Evocative of Hardy ... an exhilarating vision'
Irish Times

'A gorgeously hypnotic paean to rural England'
Guardian

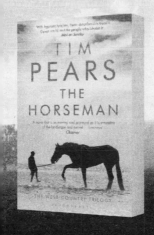
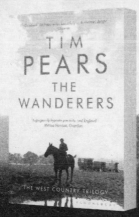
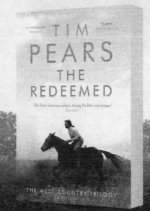

Discover the full WEST COUNTRY TRILOGY today

BLOOMSBURY